WILLIAM BUTLER YEATS

MODERN MASTERS

Already published

ALBERT CAMUS / Conor Cruise O'Brien
FRANTZ FANON / David Caute
HERBERT MARCUSE / Alasdair MacIntyre
CHE GUEVARA / Andrew Sinclair
CLAUDE LÉVI-STRAUSS / Edmund Leach
LUDWIG WITTGENSTEIN / David Pears
GEORGE LUKÁCS / George Lichtheim
NOAM CHOMSKY / John Lyons
JAMES JOYCE / John Gross
MARSHALL MCLUHAN / Jonathan Miller
GEORGE ORWELL / Raymond Williams
SIGMUND FREUD / Richard Wollheim
WILHELM REICH / Charles Rycroft

MODERN MASTERS

EDITED BY frank kermode

william
butler yeats

denis donoghue

NEW YORK | THE VIKING PRESS

ACKNOWLEDGMENTS

Alfred A. Knopf, Inc.: "Mr. Burnshaw and the Statue" from
the poem "Owl's Clover" from *Opus Posthumous*. Copyright
1937, and renewed 1965 by Holly Stevens Stephenson.
"Esthetique du Mal" from *The Collected Poems of Wallace
Stevens*. Copyright 1947 by Wallace Stevens. Reprinted by
permission of Alfred A. Knopf, Inc.
The Macmillan Company: From *A Vision* by William Butler
Yeats. Copyright 1937 by The Macmillan Company, renewed
1965 by Bertha Georgie Yeats and Anne Butler Yeats. From
Explorations by William Butler Yeats. Copyright 1937 by
The Macmillan Company, renewed 1965 by Bertha Georgie
Yeats and Anne Butler Yeats. From *Essays and Introduc-
tions* by William Butler Yeats. © by Mrs. W. B. Yeats. From
Collected Poems by William Butler Yeats. Copyright 1903,
1906, 1907, 1912, 1916, 1918, 1919, 1924, 1928, 1931, 1933,
1934, 1935, 1940, 1944, 1945, 1946, 1950, 1956 by The
Macmillan Company. Copyright 1940 by Georgie Yeats.
Copyright renewed 1931, 1934 by William Butler Yeats.
Copyright renewed 1956 by Georgie Yeats. Copyright renewed 1968 by Bertha Georgie Yeats, Michael Butler Yeats,
and Anne Yeats. Reprinted with permission of The Macmillan Company.

CONTENTS

BIOGRAPHICAL NOTE

1865   William Butler Yeats born in Dublin, son of John
        Butler Yeats and Susan Yeats.

1867   Yeats family moves to 23 Fitzroy Road, Regent's
        Park, London, to enable J.B.Y. to pursue his voca-
        tion as a portrait painter.

1872   W.B.Y. taken on extended holiday to his grand-
        parents' home in Sligo, the first of many such
        visits.

1874   Family moves to West Kensington, London.

1875–80 Attends the Godolphin School, Hammersmith,
        London.

1876   Family moves to Bedford Park, London.

1880   Family returns to Ireland, first settling at Bals-
        cadden Cottage, Howth, Co. Dublin.

1881–83 Attends the Erasmus High School, Harcourt St.,
        Dublin.

1881   Family moves to Island View, Howth. W.B.Y. now
        holidays with his uncle, George Pollexfen, in
        Sligo.

1883   W.B.Y. attends the Metropolitan School of Art,

Kildare Street, Dublin. His colleagues include the poet George W. Russell (AE) and the sculptors John Hughes and Oliver Sheppard.

1884   Family moves to 10 Ashfield Terrace, Harold's Cross, Dublin.

1885   W.B.Y.'s first publication, two short lyrics in the March issue of the *Dublin University Review*. Joins with Charles Johnston and others to form the Dublin Hermetic Society.

1886   Begins writing essays and reviews for various literary magazines.

1887   Family moves back to London. W.B.Y. joins the Theosophical Society in London.

1888   Family moves to Bedford Park, London. W.B.Y. meets Oscar Wilde, William Morris, G. B. Shaw, W. E. Henley. Compiles *Fairy and Folk Tales*.

1889   *The Wanderings of Oisin, and Other Poems*, W.B.Y.'s first book of poems, published. Meets Maud Gonne; begins intensive study of Blake's Prophetic Books.

1890   Initiated into the Hermetic Order of the Golden Dawn. In June, sees Florence Farr acting in Todhunter's *A Sicilian Idyll*.

1891   *John Sherman and Dhoya*. Death of Parnell. Foundation of the Rhymers' Club and of the Irish Literary Society.

1892   *The Countess Kathleen and Various Legends and Lyrics*.

1893   *The Celtic Twilight*. W.B.Y. edits, with Edwin J. Ellis, *The Works of William Blake*.

1894   *The Land of Heart's Desire*. W.B.Y. meets Mrs. Olivia Shakespear, a cousin of Lionel Johnson.

1895   *A Book of Irish Verse*. W.B.Y. takes rooms, with Arthur Symons, in Fountain Court, Temple, London.

1896   W.B.Y. moves to 18 Woburn Buildings. On a visit to Paris with Symons attends performance of Jarry's *Ubu Roi*. Meets J. M. Synge. Tours the west of Ireland with Symons. Meets Lady Gregory.

1897   *The Secret Rose*. W.B.Y. spends the first of many summers at Coole Park, Lady Gregory's home.

1899   *The Wind among the Reeds*. W.B.Y. proposes marriage to Maud Gonne, unsuccessfully.

1900   W.B.Y.'s mother dies. W.B.Y. becomes head of London Branch of the Order of the Golden Dawn.

1902   Family returns to Ireland. W.B.Y.'s younger sister Elizabeth starts the Dun Emer Press (later called the Cuala Press). W.B.Y. meets James Joyce. Irish National Theatre Society founded with W.B.Y. as President.

1903   *In the Seven Woods*. Also *Ideas of Good and Evil*. In February, Maud Gonne marries Major John MacBride. *The King's Threshold*. W.B.Y. goes on lecture tour to the United States.

1904   Abbey Theatre gives its first performance (December 27); the bill includes *On Baile's Strand*.

1906   W.B.Y., Lady Gregory, and Synge appointed directors of the Abbey Theatre. First performance of Yeats's *Deirdre* (November 26). *Poems 1899–1905*.

1907   Public controversy arising from turbulent first performance of Synge's *The Playboy of the Western World*. With Lady Gregory and her son Robert, W.B.Y. spends the spring on Italian holiday. J.B.Y. sails for New York.

1908   W.B.Y. meets Ezra Pound.

1909   Death of Synge (March 24). W.B.Y. edits Synge's *Poems and Translations*.

1910   *The Green Helmet, and Other Poems*. W.B.Y. awarded Civil List yearly pension of £150 with proviso that he is free to take part in political activities in Ireland.

1911   Meets Miss George Hyde-Lees.

1912   Meets the Indian poet Tagore. *The Cutting of an Agate*.

1913   Takes rooms "at Stone Cottage in Sussex by the waste moor" (Pound's description). Pound acts as secretary while editing Ernest Fenollosa's translations of Noh plays. *Poems Written in Discouragement*.

1914   *Responsibilities*. W.B.Y. goes on lecture tour in the United States.

1915   Death of Hugh Lane on the *Lusitania*, followed by public controversy over the legal disposition of his collection of Impressionist paintings.

1916   The Easter Rising. John MacBride executed. W.B.Y. buys Norman tower at Ballylee, near Coole, and plans to restore it and live there in summer. *At the Hawk's Well* performed in London.

1917   Proposes marriage to Iseult Gonne, Maud Gonne's daughter, unsuccessfully. Marries George Hyde-Lees (October 20). *The Wild Swans at Coole*.

1918   *Per Amica Silentia Lunae. The Only Jealousy of Emer.*

1919   W.B.Y.'s daughter Anne Butler Yeats born (February 26).

1920   W.B.Y. on lecture tour in the United States. On return, lives at Oxford. *Michael Robartes and the Dancer*.

1921   W.B.Y. and family living at Shillingford, Berkshire. In August, they move to Thame, Oxfordshire. Son born on August 22, William Michael Yeats.

1922   *The Trembling of the Veil*. J.B.Y. dies in New York. W.B.Y. and family move to 82 Merrion Square, Dublin. W.B.Y. accepts invitation to become a member of the first Irish Senate, with office until 1928. In the Irish Civil War his sympathies are on the pro-Treaty side, and he opposes the Republicans.

1923   Receives the Nobel Prize for Literature.

1924   W.B.Y. and his wife holiday in Sicily and Italy (November).

1925   W.B.Y.'s Senate speech on Divorce (June 11). First version of *A Vision* published.

1926   W.B.Y.'s translation of *Oedipus Rex* produced at the Abbey. W.B.Y. becomes Chairman of the Committee to advise the Minister for Finance on suitable coinage for Ireland.

1927   W.B.Y., recovering from lung congestion, goes for holiday to Algeciras, Seville, and Cannes.

1928   W.B.Y. at Rapallo. In April, returns to Dublin. Returns to Rapallo. *The Tower* published.

1929   Suffers attack of Maltese fever. *Fighting the Waves* performed in Dublin.

1930   Back in Dublin (July).

1931   Divides the year between Dublin, Coole, and Oxford.

1932   Death of Lady Gregory. W.B.Y. moves to Riversdale, Rathfarnham, Dublin, his last home in Ireland. Goes on lecture tour in the United States.

1933   *The Winding Stair.*

1934   *Wheels and Butterflies.*

1935   *A Full Moon in March.* Meets Lady Gerald Wellesley.

1936   Goes to Majorca, accompanied by the Indian Swami Shri Purohit. Returns to Dublin in June. *The Oxford Book of Modern Verse* published.

1937   Revised version of *A Vision.*

1938   For his health's sake, W.B.Y. goes to Menton, then to Cap Martin. First performance of *Purgatory* (August). *The Herne's Egg.* At work on *The Death of Cuchulain.*

1939   W.B.Y. dies (January 28). Buried at Roquebrune. (The war prevented his burial in Ireland. In 1948 his remains were returned to Ireland and buried at Drumcliff, Sligo.)

WILLIAM BUTLER YEATS

Introduction: Toward the Poetry

I should explain at once what I hope to do in this book, if only because the justification of publishing a study of Yeats at this time cannot be self-evident. There are many books on the subject already. Besides, my book has nothing new to offer in any of the following respects: it is not a biography, not even a "brief life"; it is not a guide to Yeats's poetry, poem by poem; it does not study the poet's sources. I am indeed concerned with the context of feeling from which the poems emerge, but I have not assumed that such a context can be indicated merely by attention to political or literary history. Yeats's sensibility is my theme, so far as it manifests itself in the poems and plays. I would be happy to think that my account of the sensibility gives at least an impression of the sustaining context, but perhaps I should stop short of that claim; it is excessive.

Readers who believe that literature is important normally believe that Yeats is important. Critics who comment on his poems generally do so in that belief, and they think of their readers as for the most part people of similar conviction. There have been dissenting voices: critics who reject the common view that Yeats is a major poet. But even they address their readers on the assumptions, presumed to be shared by reader and critic, that the imagination is most profoundly engaged in literature, and that among the several kinds of literature a special aura surrounds poetry as the most subtle and concentrated life of language. Such critics deny that Yeats was a great poet, but they are among the first to assert that poetry is crucial in the history of the imagination. The late Yvor Winters was a critic of that persuasion. When he discussed Yeats's poems, he assumed that the question of poetry was a supreme question, and he argued his case with that grandeur in mind. He took for granted that his readers were of like mind, so far as the nature and value of poetry were in question.

But it is my impression that Yeats's readers nowadays include many people who have not felt obliged to make a grand commitment to poetry in general or to literature once for all. These readers do not assert the primacy of literature; they are not convinced that the imagination acts more profoundly in literature than in anthropology, philosophy, linguistics, the documentary film, or the social sciences. Mostly, literary critics preach to the converted, and their chief care is to avoid scandalizing the faithful. It is a new and tonic experience to address readers who retain, as they say, an open mind on their allegiances. In the short run, such readers make a critic's life harder; they ask improbable questions, make wild leaps from one thing to another, propose conjunctions and fancies hardly certified in the academy. But over a longer stretch the critic is likely to feel exhilarated by the novel experience.

It cannot be impertinent to begin by saying that Yeats was a poet. He might have been mistaken for something else: politician, orator, theosophist, journalist, "public man." He helped to found the Abbey Theatre, committing himself to "theatre business, management of men." He invented a country, calling it Ireland. An enthusiast of vision, he conspired with mages, meditating upon "unknown thought." But he took up these interests as latent forms of poetry, and the attention he gave them was poetic. Activities won his affection when they showed themselves capable of being brought to the condition of poetry. His life, seemingly diverse if not disheveled, was unified by this consideration: everything ministered to his imagination, and was judged by that law. When Yeats became an Irish Senator, Ezra Pound twitted him for reviving the ancient art of oratory, but Yeats knew that a speech may be a poetic act. A speech has only this disability, compared with a poem: that its survival depends upon memory and tradition and is therefore precarious. The poetic imagination has many aspects and relations. We say that it is creative, meaning that it delights in fiction, it runs beyond the empirical evidence. Yeats accepted this sense of the word, but he added a further consideration, that imagination is a poet's conscience. To deal with ordinary things imaginatively is to deal with them somewhat strictly; it is not to play ducks and drakes with them. Certainly a poet is strict with himself on these occasions; he must satisfy his imagination, whether the formal result is a poem, a public speech, or a letter to a newspaper. It has sometimes been maintained that

Yeats's professional care was given to verse and that his remaining interests were merely vacation exercises to beguile the time. The argument is intended to make the reader look carelessly upon these amateur pursuits, forgiving them when they irritate him. The poem is the thing. But a stronger argument says that there is no division between professional and amateur care. Yeats sought to make himself a poet—that is, to transform his experience, composing his life as if it were a poem. Experience provided the themes, the poetic matter, and imagination worked over this material, drawing it to definition and form. A man's life is one thing and then another; a poet's life is his *Collected Poems*. Yeats sought to make his entire life an *oeuvre*: the more diverse the material, the better. "Pure Poetry" was not his aim.

It was a formidable intention. Generally, poets are willing to settle for less, dividing their lives into amateur and professional occasions, with somewhat different requirements for each category. But we have only to read a few of Yeats's poems to sense in them an exorbitant ambition. The poems may be wise, charming, and so forth, but they have these qualities by chance rather than intention. The character upon which Yeats's art is directed, with a poet's intensity, is power: it denotes mastery, self-mastery if the self is in question, as it regularly is. Going through the *Collected Poems*, a reader of Yeats finds himself living in an empire of feeling; the characteristic styles are imperial, words for the music of trumpets. Gradually the sense of present power imposes itself, and the reader finds himself taking everything in that spirit. Perhaps he is impressionable. But it is remarkable how persuasive the spirit is and how determinedly Yeats's poems draw an entire life—his own—

toward a center of power, whether its official name passion, energy, will, or imagination. The life is various and eventful in its own right, but it is not allowed to press a claim until the formal requirements of the poem are satisfied. The relation between feeling and form is not allowed to run loose. If Yeats's poems have a common style, it may be recognized by this sign: that it treats the relation between experience and poetry as that of servant and master. The reader, too, is kept in his place; demeanor is important because the relation between poet and reader is severe. It is not required of this style that it humble itself in order to be forgiven. The words are tokens of authority, and the only choice available to the reader is to accept or reject them. When we feel that a poem by Yeats is arrogant, we recognize the terms in which it is offered and we think them offensive. It is a requirement that we bend the knee. But arrogance is merely the extreme limit of his common tone: the sense of power is the most pervasive sense at work in the poems.

More specifically, I would maintain that Yeats delights in conflict, because it is a mode of power. His imagination loves to cause trouble, starting quarrels between one value and another. His mind is restless with finality, because finality is peace or death. Those who say that Yeats was a Platonist are right, subject to the qualification that he was the opposite, empiricist or realist, even on the same occasions. If we select a value and say it is dear to Yeats, we may be right, but only if we allow equal recognition to its opposite. There are indeed official preferences, but Yeats values above all the energy of conflict. His mind needs two terms, one hardly less compelling than the other: action and knowledge, essence and existence, power and wisdom, imagination and will, life and word, personality and character, drama and picture, vision and reality. Any one of these may engage his feeling, but the feeling longs to touch its opposite; the pairs are entertained for the tension they engender, the energy they release. It is foolish, then, to recruit Yeats to a cause; he will go over to the enemy, if only to prolong the quarrel. Now it is a maxim of criticism that a poet does not speak in his own but in an assumed character. Every poet is in that measure a dramatic poet; he imagines feelings and situations different from his own. But Yeats took this general truth more intimately to heart, making the dramatic imagination the productive force of his life. He thought of experience as, potentially, a dramatic poem: circumstance the matter, conflict and imagination the instruments, poetry the end. As for truth itself, he believed that it could not be stated, could not be known, but might be enacted. Truth lives in the mode of action, not of knowledge: it is enacted in the temporal form of the play, and only that form is true.

In a later chapter I shall say something about a resplendent pair, history and symbol, arguing of Yeats's symbolism that it accepts the intervention of history with regret; and of his historical sense that it longs to yield to the purity of presence, the present tense and that alone. These categories are familiar and therefore obscure—as obscure as other categories which they resemble, existence and essence, time and eternity. For corresponding techniques, I distinguish between interpretation and divination, the first for the historical signs, the second for symbolic portents. We make the same distinction between historicism and structuralism: historicism respects the social grammar of beginning, middle, and an end not yet reached, its congenial art is narrative; structuralism has no time for history and respects only the internal force of structure, considered as a natural law removed from time and place. I am not sure that it would be fruitless to drive our pairs somewhat further, thinking of two corresponding forms of power, politics and magic. Under any name, each member of these several pairs has its sponsors: the arguments for and against structuralism make a case in point. It would be idle to say that these merely make a quarrel or that the imagination has no place among them. But one thing can be said: that each participant takes up his position and defends it relentlessly. He does not disclose misgiving, doubt, subversive qualms, occult allegiance to his enemy. I think a greater power of imagination is manifested where, as in Yeats's case, the rivalries are proposed and pursued within the same mind. The trouble about a quarrel, where two men quarrel, is that each hunts the other long past reason. When the quarrels are pursued within the same mind, the pursuit may still be intense but it is war to the life, not to the death, and the greatest cause is acknowledged to be life itself—energy, vitality.

Historically, Yeats may be understood within the context of European Romanticism. We acknowledge this when we respond to his work in terms of imagination, self and world, image and symbol, or when we think of idealism as its philosophical companion. In its general bearing, the work may be related to the preoccupations of the European mind since Blake, Kant, Wordsworth, and Goethe. The context is then clarified if it is allowed to include Symbolism as a special case of Romanticism, a case most suggestively present in Mallarmé and other French poets. If the matter were to be dealt with in social and political terms, it would be necessary to think of Ireland as a special case of Europe: Yeats's own words would take the harm out of the extravagance. But if he is placed without further ado in the general setting of European Romanticism, even allowing for special cases, something is missing. I think it is the theatrical element, the sense of life as action and gesture. Before the context of feeling is really useful, it must contain something active, individualistic, harsh, intolerant. To mark this element I emphasize Yeats's kinship with Nietzsche: it seems to me a more telling relation than that between Yeats and Plato, Plotinus, or Blake.

The general sense of Yeats's work that I propose depends upon certain notions that are easy to recite but hard to define. I mean such notions as self, imagination, will, action, symbol, history, world, vision, self-transformation. I cannot define these terms in any way that would please a strict reader. Some of them are reasonably clear, I think, in their practical employment, but I shall make some primitive notes about them here. The idea of self-transformation is implicit in any Romanticism that takes itself seriously, where imagination is deemed a creative faculty and the self its final concern. One of the crucial doctrines of Romanticism is that the self is free, and freely creative: imagination is the common name for that freedom. The Romantic imagination is understood as exercising its freedom by playing widely ranging roles in a continuous drama: the poet is playwright and actor in his own play. The self is the object of its own attention: the attention, we say, is reflexive. The self, in another version, creates and extends itself by a continuous act of imagination; thus it evades the penury of the given. Romantic insistence upon the creative power of imagination has often appeared pretentious, but it is a reaction against the forces of positivism which deny the self its freedom. I have such a quarrel in mind when I refer to this motif in Yeats. By symbol I mean whatever

Yeats means when he can be quoted in point; otherwise I mean any natural form or event which has acquired special significance by virtue of the ancestral feeling that has gathered about it. The symbol is spontaneously evocative. By history I mean the past as an object of imaginative care, or as that in time which resists the imagination, however unsuccessfully. World may be taken to mean things as they are or even as they appear to a common glance; I do not make a severe definition. Vision is what an artist sees with the mind's eye; it is an internal power, often stimulated by an object in nature but not limited to a recital of the qualities deemed to belong to that object. Vision may refer to this power, or to its more or less fictive productions; it is hardly to be distinguished from the *fiat* of the imagination.

Readers of Yeats must decide how far they are willing to go to meet him, and in what directions; his work bears upon modern feeling in several categories—poetry, drama, criticism, politics, social history, philosophy, religion, magic. I shall try to indicate the directions that seem most productive.

A Kind of Power

●

1

In 1937, two years before his death, W. B. Yeats wrote "A General Introduction for My Work," announcing as his first principle that a poet "is never the bundle of accident and incoherence that sits down to breakfast." A poet is not merely, like the man at the breakfast table, the sum of his experiences. Between the man and the poet there is always, as Yeats said, a phantasmagoria; we think of it when we advert to the form of a poem, the role a poet plays, or the transfiguring power of imagination. Wallace Stevens's word for the same thing is "hallucination." A man is simply a man, and according to some moralists that condition is enough; he lacks nothing. But Yeats ascribed to the poet—"more type than man, more passion than type"—the power of transformation: the poet can make himself anew, become his own God, as Nietzsche said

Goethe created himself, by the imperative act of his imagination. He can turn accident into design, animate what mere experience has left inert. In the power of imagination, Yeats wrote, "nature has grown intelligible, and by so doing a part of our creative power."[1] The message is characteristic of Yeats in several respects; it defines his sense of art as compensation for the chaos of personal life; it expresses his hierarchical feeling for the poet as seer, bringing nature to form and definition; above all, it marks his recourse to the imagination of power. Yeats's major poems are correlatives of power, their personality attested in a certain tone of voice; he wrote as if he were leading a charge of cavalry. We recognize his style by its tone of command; often, in its presence, we stand rebuked.

It is my impression that Yeats's struggle toward an "answerable style" and his determination to achieve self-mastery are versions of the same motive; language is the enabling instrument. He does not speak, as T. S. Eliot does, of separating the man who suffers from the writer who creates; or if he seems to, his intonation is entirely different. Eliot would use art to suppress the demanding self; the suffering man confides his experience to the poetic form, remaining silent in his own person. The separation Eliot proposes is the poetic equivalent of humility, its motive is ascetic: "humility is endless." But Yeats's phantasmagoria comes from a conviction of his poetic power, a promise of forces to be invoked. Life and work are not the same, their perfections are distinguishable and often at odds, there is always a phantasmagoria. That is to say, there is always the imagination. It is a mark of Yeats's achievement that his greatest work con-

[1] *Essays and Introductions*, p. 509.

tains within itself the reasons why it is such and not other; the integrity of the poems means that they do not need, for elucidation, the remote charm of biography. The four or five poems that turn chapters of *A Vision* into verse are demonstrably not those on which his reputation depends. But, so much conceded, Yeats was nonchalant in driving life and work together. He made his poetic coat out of old mythologies, but also out of daily occasions, the chances of ordinary life, abrasions of love and hate. There is risk in referring poetry to the breakfast table, but in this case the risk is worth taking, he took it in his own behalf, he did not choose to be anonymous. The youth who first saw power in his father, John Butler Yeats, and then took his bundle of accident and incoherence to another man of power, John O'Leary, was already playing what he felt to be a predestined part: only its particular lineaments had yet to be discovered. With hindsight, the only reliable form of wisdom, we can see how the patterns of life and art correspond and feel the tension between them.

Yeats was born on June 13, 1865, in the house which is now 5 Sandymount Avenue, Dublin. His father was then a law student, and was soon to become a barrister, but eventually an artist, a portrait painter. His mother, formerly Susan Pollexfen, was the daughter of a prosperous merchant in Sligo. Yeats chose to think that his paternal ancestors had been influential people, and in "Reveries over Childhood and Youth" he professed himself "delighted with all that joins my life to those who had power in Ireland";[2] he was already making a myth by which the poet might live. His grandfather, John Yeats, had been a Protestant rector in County Down; to

[2] *Autobiographies*, p. 22.

come upon power it was necessary to search further among the generations. In the prefatory poem to *Responsibilities* Yeats lays claim to "blood / That has not passed through any huckster's loin," a sentiment fundamental to his sense of race and power. The connection with the Pollexfens was somewhat embarrassing: they were well-respected people but considered "purse-proud," and Yeats was easy with them only when they displayed the saving graces, a taste for astrology, prowess in horsemanship, the "wasteful virtues" which alone "earn the sun." He recalled his father saying, "When I was young, the definition of a gentleman was a man not wholly occupied in getting on."[3] Normally, Yeats would have been expected to identify himself with the Anglo-Irish tradition and with that alone, but he did not. When he went to school in London he felt himself a stranger, his mind filled with Irish images. But in Ireland he was separated from the historical traditions available to him: from the Catholics because he could not share their faith and he deplored their taste; from the Protestant Ascendancy for different but equally compelling reasons. "I had noticed," he writes, "that Irish Catholics among whom had been born so many political martyrs had not the good taste, the household courtesy and decency of the Protestant Ireland I had known, yet Protestant Ireland seemed to think of nothing but getting on in the world."[4] Besides, Protestant Ireland, considered as an institution of power, was obviously in decline. So there was no question of his committing himself to either of these traditions, although he maintained links with each. He revered the Protestant Ascendancy so long as it manifested itself in Swift, Burke, Grattan, Goldsmith, Molyneux, Berkeley, "no

[3] *Ibid.*, p. 90.
[4] *Ibid.*, p. 102.

petty people." But this great tradition had now fallen into the hands of Trinity College and Professor Dowden, in Yeats's eyes the last guardians of "West Britonism." The next turn of the historical cycle seemed to favor the other tradition, largely Catholic and often Gaelic. Yeats supported those patriotic movements which he could reconcile with the strict demands of his taste: the Gaelic League, and other national associations. But he was a somewhat Tory Nationalist. He admired Douglas Hyde, though he rebuked him for maintaining that the soul of Ireland spoke only in Irish. Yeats was interested in the Irish language, short of actually learning it, but he could not endorse Hyde's exclusive rhetoric. He envied Hyde his familiar relation to the Irish people: "You've dandled them and fed them from the book / And know them to the bone." But he saw that he himself could never become, like Hyde in Ireland, "most popular of men."

Born and reared between two communities, Yeats could not find himself in either, so he sought a tradition deeper than Catholic or Protestant yet native to the spirit of Ireland and more profound, he thought, than either of its great historical versions. He identified himself with that hidden Ireland for which the available evidence is an anthropology of customs, beliefs, and holy places. Many of his early essays and reviews, beginning in 1886, are attempts to persuade that Ireland to reveal itself, now that its time has come. There is a direct relation between Yeats's calling upon the hidden Ireland to come forth, by myth and personification, and his effort to define himself as a poet. The same imaginative idiom applies to both. Yeats's Ireland is a fiction; so is his Poet.

What Yeats wanted is clear enough when he writes of Hyde, Thomas Davis, or Parnell: a powerful relation to "the people." When he read Davis's poems and other work from *The Nation*, he saw that they were poor things, and he rejected their bombast, but those poets, he said, "had one quality I admired and admire: they were not separated individual men; they spoke or tried to speak out of a people to a people; behind them stretched the generations."[5] In the account of Phase 10 of *A Vision*, where Parnell is the example, Yeats writes of "a kind of burning restraint, a something that suggests a savage statue to which one offers sacrifice." He continues, "This sacrifice is code, personality no longer perceived as power only. He seeks by its help to free the creative power from mass emotion, but never wholly succeeds, and so the life remains troubled, a conflict between pride and race, and passes from crisis to crisis."[6] There are differences: Hyde is a popular man; Davis speaks in the voice of simple, strong, perhaps crude feeling; Parnell exemplifies the lonely man of pride. But they are all, in their different ways, men of power, and Yeats responded to them for that capacity. Nearer home, there was Lady Gregory, a commanding person, Anglo-Irish gentry but deeply devoted to "the people." Yeats saw in her the possibility of gaining the best of both worlds; knowing the texture of common life without abandoning the pride of station that Lady Gregory represented. Her work in Irish folklore was crucial in this way because lore was, in Yeats's phrase, "the book of the people." The feelings and beliefs assembled in Lady Gregory's *Cuchulain of Muirthemne, Gods and Fighting Men*, and *Visions and Beliefs in the West of Ireland* were indisputably Irish, and they came from a source deeper than any Church: they were made by men and women who, having nothing to lose, had nothing to fear. The stories were hospit-

[5] *Essays and Introductions*, p. 510.
[6] *A Vision*, p. 123.

able to miracle, the occult, and magic; they seemed to promise a revelation, if only their energy could be gathered, and Yeats hoped to gather some of it in his plays of Cuchulain. Jorge Luis Borges has written that "music, states of happiness, mythology, faces belaboured by time, certain twilights and certain places try to tell us something, or have said something we should have missed, or are about to say something; this imminence of a revelation which does not occur is, perhaps, the aesthetic phenomenon."[7]

In the years before and after the publication of *The Celtic Twilight* (1893) Yeats was waiting for a revelation, the veil was already trembling, but the revelation he sought must take an aesthetic form; in the theater perhaps, in a London séance, or in the soul of a nation revealed as gesture. In 1886 he appealed "to those young men clustered here and there throughout our land, whom the emotion of Patriotism has lifted into that world of selfless passion in which heroic deeds are possible and heroic poetry credible."[8] If "great nations blossom above," as he wrote in a late poem, they blossom in people like Lady Gregory, not only in men of great power. Lady Gregory's strength was her pride, nourished by contact with ancestral feeling, memories, visions, customs, transmitted like songs and stories. She was also, in the moral sense, a leader.

It was not a question of practical power. Yeats has sometimes been accused of harboring political designs, sinister ambitions, as if he planned to become Ireland's Mussolini. The charge is null. There is no evidence, even

[7] Jorge Luis Borges, *Labyrinths*, eds. Donald A. Yates and James E. Irby (London, 1970), p. 223. This piece translated by Irby.
[8] *Uncollected Prose*, p. 104.

in his years as a senator, that he wanted high office or that if it had come, however improbably, into his hands he would have used it violently. He wanted moral power, self-mastery, self-definition. For himself, all ambitions came down to one: to transform his own experience. In an essay on Berkeley he said that the Romantic movement had been superseded by a new naturalism "that leaves man helpless before the contents of his own mind";[9] the only power Yeats wanted was command over that mass. In *A Vision* he offered *The Tower* and *The Winding Stair* as evidence that, in some measure, he had achieved what he sought.

But laws of evidence vary from one culture to another. In Ireland, where the governing art is rhetoric, proof of power is voice. Irish history is elucidated not in books but in speeches; hence the reverberation of the Cyclops episode in Joyce's *Ulysses*. Hence, too, the value ascribed to gesture. In "All Things Can Tempt Me" Yeats writes:

> When I was young,
> I had not given a penny for a song
> Did not the poet sing it with such airs
> That one believed he had a sword upstairs.

Even when a book is allowed, it must be "a written speech / Wrought of high laughter, loveliness and ease." The danger in this tradition is that a man will give himself the airs he lacks, and there are some late poems, such as "Under Ben Bulben," in which Yeats is too generous in that cause. But for better or worse he committed himself to rhetoric. Invariably the "beautiful lofty things" he celebrates are speeches, gestures, "my father upon the Abbey stage, before him a raging crowd," Standish

[9] *Essays and Introductions*, p. 405.

O'Grady speaking to a drunken audience in "high non-sensical words." Nonsense does not matter, so the words be fine. Margot Ruddock, the "crazed girl" of Yeats's *Last Poems*, is recalled dancing upon the shore, wound "in desperate music," beautiful, because her soul is declared in a splendid gesture. In gesture there is no distinction between content and form: gesture is the dance of attitude.

To Yeats, tradition is oral, the continuity of voice from generation to generation. In a visual culture experience is understood as a field of reference, and the important events are those which alter the configuration of the whole, changing the perspective. "The eye altering alters all." T. S. Eliot described tradition in this sense in his "Tradition and the Individual Talent," where masterpieces are deployed like monuments and tradition is a visual relation. In a visual culture the "point of view" is crucial, and the fundamental question is the relation between subject and object. Seeing is believing. But in an oral culture—and Yeats's Ireland was one of its farewell performances—experience is speech, lore, rumor, anecdote, the tale rather than the novel. *Finnegans Wake* has Roderick O'Connor talking "earish with his eyes shut." "In Ireland today," Yeats wrote in "Literature and the Living Voice," "the old world that sang and listened is, it may be for the last time in Europe, face to face with the world that reads and writes, and their antagonism is always present under some name or other in Irish imagination and intellect."[10] His own fictive Ireland becomes an antithetical hero opposed to the primary force of England, the force of "Ireland" in that relation being consonant with the power of poetry. So Yeats's antagonism

[10] *Explorations*, p. 206.

is directed against "the literature of the 'point of view,' " product of isolation and the printing press. In his poems he sought "syntax that is for ear alone"; he wanted the Abbey Theatre to be a place for nuances of voice, and for the correspondingly national feeling. He thought of tradition, in its bearing upon Ireland, as an *anima Hiberniae*, "emotion of multitude" released as an endless tale, motifs, sounds, echoes, the whole "story of the night" deeper, more profound, than those parts of it which are merely Christian or merely pagan. In the "General Introduction" he speaks of "a Christ posed against a background not of Judaism but of Druidism, not shut off in dead history, but flowing, concrete, phenomenal." "I was born into this faith," he adds, "have lived in it, and shall die in it; my Christ, a legitimate deduction from the Creed of St. Patrick as I think, is that Unity of Being Dante compared to a perfectly proportioned human body, Blake's 'Imagination,' what the Upanishads have named 'Self.' "[11] Tradition was a measure of that Unity of Culture which Yeats invoked to sustain individual Unity of Being.

Nothing in Yeats's concept of tradition intimidates his sense of power. It could be argued that his version of tradition respected only race and had little care for society. Man's two eternities are "that of race and that of soul." Yeats speaks of man, not of men; his mind turns unwillingly to detail, unless the detail is a nuance of feeling. He admired notable people, but his respect for ordinary people as constituting a particular society and living a certain life at a certain time was extremely weak; when he looked beyond the chosen few he saw a fictive race rather than a finite society. He did not think of collective consciousness as the sum of states of individual

[11] *Essays and Introductions*, p. 518.

consciousness—a Marxist criterion described by Lucien Goldmann in *Sciences Humaines et Philosophie*; for Yeats, beyond society there was always race, beyond the sum of individual minds Mind itself, beyond the sum of states of individual subconsciousness the *anima mundi*. Arithmetic was an alien science. It is significant that Yeats disliked the nineteenth-century novel, except for Balzac, whom he revered for the Swedenborgian symbolism: it is hard to think of Yeats as a reader of *Middlemarch*. When he writes of society, it seems to consist of invisible men, and it is remarkable if he inquires into their lives, works, and days, how they make a living, what they think and feel. But his imagination is stirred when the theme is race, kindred, blood, consanguinity, "the fury and the mire of human veins" or "honey of generation." Yeats responded to life when it had reached the pitch of definition, or when it could be brought to such a pitch; and only those moments really counted. He did not conclude that life between those holy moments was a waste sad time without vitality or form, but rather that the intervals were null, because they were not transfigured by a sufficient imagination; no poet had been present to redeem them. This is largely Pater's legacy to Yeats, the sense of life as aspiring to certain moments of intensity, the flame, "the fire that makes all simple," the "blaze" of Yeats's "Vacillation," the conflagration of "In Memory of Major Robert Gregory." It also explains the impression, in Yeats's early poems, of nature as a heap of broken images, discontinuous, uncharted; of an abyss between one privileged moment and another. Symbolism offered the possibility of establishing a continuous life of energy at a level beneath that of time and history, but it did not help Yeats to understand his own moment in historical experience.

In fact, Yeats hoped to blur the distinction between history and myth, thinking rather of moments certified by feeling. In *A Vision* the definitive moments in history are identified with certain great men, heroes because they answered their time with a masterly imagination. Historical events counted for less than the heroic energy that they provoked: events were exalted by the heroes who enacted them. For the grand rhythm of feeling, however, history was not enough, Yeats needed archetypal figures released from history—the Fool, the Harlot, the Hunchback, the King. Such figures were required because they embodied certain perennial motives and visions, heroic in the clarity of their definition. The equivalent of the Poet, in this way, was the Mage, man of power. Speaking of religion and magic in the Epilogue to *Per Amica Silentia Lunae*, Yeats says, "Have not my thoughts run through a like round, though I have not found my tradition in the Catholic Church, which was not the Church of my childhood, but where the tradition is, as I believe, more universal and more ancient?"[12] The doctrines of this tradition are given in "Ideas of Good and Evil": first, that the "borders of our mind are ever shifting, and that many minds can flow into one another, as it were, and create or reveal a single mind, a single energy"; second, "that the borders of our memories are as shifting, and that our memories are a part of one great memory, the memory of Nature herself"; and third, "that this great mind and great memory can be evoked by symbols."[13] In this tradition there is no obstacle between the individual mind and the *anima mundi* to and from which it flows. If the Catholic Church claims truth, Yeats's church claims wisdom and power, an immensely rich

[12] *Mythologies*, pp. 368–69.
[13] *Essays and Introductions*, p. 28.

treasure of images, icons, symbols. Every mind is priest in its own ceremonies, offering sacrifice, entering into communion with the living dead, interpreting the esoteric signs. The adept, like the poet, seeks an image.

In reading Yeats, then, we are not obliged to separate ourselves from his magic, from the "harsh geometry" of *A Vision*, from those preoccupations to which W. H. Auden condescended as the southern Californian element in Yeats. Magic and poetry are forms of power, and they have often been kin. Besides, I am not sure that Yeats's belief in the *anima mundi* is more fanciful than a philosopher's belief in innate ideas, a geneticist's belief in heredity, or a linguist's belief in a child's possession of generative grammar. The mage seeks an image, the poet's imagination seeks a form, the bundle of accident and incoherence seeks lucidity: three manifestations of a single motive; unity of action, diversity of content. We have no difficulty accepting the third, since it is common in its aim and notable only in its means; or the second, which is the imaginative search at any time. If we disengage ourselves from the first aim, it is because we renounce all that is not history, politics, or sociology; or we resent a doctrine which takes hold of experience by ritual; or we denounce priestly craft as witch medicine. These reactions will serve a turn, but none is convincing.

The most resolute charge to be brought against Yeats is that he consorted with the archaic, but if we bring the charge we delude ourselves. What we resent is that he sought companionship among occult images. The case is clear. Instead of endorsing our politics, he made an archaic aesthetic, drawn from occasions imperial rather than liberal or democratic, Italian more often than Irish or English. Instead of our religion, he gathered a fardel of old stories, legends, beliefs established "before Christ was crucified" and never entirely abandoned. Instead of our psychology, he consulted horoscopes, patterns, Brancusi forms, coincidences. But it would be vain to conclude that his rhetoric, because it resorts to archaic materials, does not bear upon our modern lives, or that we can deflect its force by calling it archaic. Yeats's willfulness is his modernity; the poems relate themselves to our time by affronting it. Yeats does not accept the modern world as his conscience; his imagination is his sole law. He thinks little of an object until it conspires with his latent powers, delivering them: so R. P. Blackmur called him "an erotic poet, with regard to his objects, not a sacramental poet."[14] A sacramental poet respects the object for itself but even more for the spirit which, however mysteriously, it contains. At some extreme point in his relation to the object, such a poet is always willing to "let be"; he is merely the spirit's celebrant. An erotic poet may respect the object in itself, but it is not characteristic of him to do so, and beyond the point of acknowledgment the only relevant spirit is his own and he is never willing to let be. When the erotic poet has done with the object, he may persist in his relation to it, but for his own sake: the object has helped him to define his power, and he is tender toward it for that reason. The distinction holds only for extreme cases; its relevance to Yeats is that a poet who resorts to the idiom of power has to decide, on tendentious occasions, whether his imagination comes first and the natural object second in his favor, or vice versa. Yeats would

[14] R. P. Blackmur, *Anni Mirabiles 1921–1925* (Washington, 1956), p. 38.

like to avoid such occasions, but if he must face them he strikes out for power, and the natural object must fend for itself.

The first evidence of Yeats's struggle for self-mastery comes in his early poems and plays. Many of them declare a world of ease beyond time, liberating the defeated lover from chains of duty and circumstance. The poet calls his lost beloved ("white woman") to "numberless islands and many a Danaan shore," preparing a scene in accordance with his sorrow, the defunctive music now fading toward a "gentle silence." There is no hope, only a dream song addressed to eternity, the state of heroic loss made permanent, ideal, essential. History and "the despotism of fact" are sublimed away. Many of these poems are beautiful; some are so fragile that they afflict the mind as murmurs from death's door. What Yeats said of late nineteenth-century poetry applies to much of his own early work. "At once the fault and the beauty of the nature-description of most modern poets is that for them the stars, and streams, the leaves, and the animals are only masks behind which go on the sad soliloquies of a nineteenth-century egoism."[15] He was severe upon himself, too. In 1888 he said that his poetry was "almost all a flight into fairyland from the real world, and a summons to that flight . . . the poetry . . . of longing and complaint—the cry of the heart against necessity," and he promised himself that he would one day write "poetry of insight and knowledge."[16]

But he had many promises to keep. He was already promised to Symbolism, which he interpreted, mainly

[15] *Uncollected Prose*, p. 103.
[16] *Letters*, p. 63.

under the impact of Arthur Symons's translations of Mallarmé, as if its only home were fairyland. In "The Symbolism of Poetry" (1900) he considered the change of poetic style that would follow if readers were to accept the theory "that poetry moves us because of its symbolism." It would mean, he said, "that we would cast out of serious poetry those energetic rhythms, as of a man running, which are the invention of the will with its eyes always on something to be done or undone; and we would seek out those wavering, meditative, organic rhythms, which are the embodiment of the imagination, that neither desires nor hates, because it has done with time, and only wishes to gaze upon some reality, some beauty."[17] The reality, like the beauty, is ideal; it scorns the empirical. Yeats's early poems are sometimes pitied rather than read: they are so delicate, so fragile, that it seems brutal to test them severely. But in fact they come from a highly sophisticated theory of Symbolism and from experiences which demanded that theory and that practice. The poems may be read as errors of judgment, but not as failures to achieve some other kind of poetry.

They are also consistent with the kinship between poetry and magic; with the interpretation of alchemy, too, outlined in *Rosa Alchemica* and elsewhere. Alchemists—*"les alchimistes, nos ancêtres,"* as Mallarmé said—sought to fashion gold from common metals, Yeats wrote, "merely as part of a universal transmutation of all things into some divine and imperishable substance." This was his justification for making *Rosa Alchemica* "a fanciful reverie over the transmutation of life into art, and a cry of measureless desire for a world

[17] *Essays and Introductions*, p. 163.

made wholly of essences."[18] In 1895 he spoke of "moods" in the same spirit. Literature is "wrought about a mood, or a community of moods, as the body is wrought about an invisible soul." Whatever the poet uses is merely an existential means, as it were, to an essential end: his purpose is "to discover immortal moods in mortal desires, an undecaying hope in our trivial ambitions, a divine love in sexual passion."[19]

The poetic problem was to make a masterful style without denying or even compromising Yeats's doctrine of Symbolism. It might be impossible, because the doctrine is remarkably pallid, and it often appears as if words were too crude a medium for transmutation and essence. But there are two moments especially in the early poems which mark important stages in the attempt. The first is "The Secret Rose" (1896). The rose is an incorrigible symbol in Yeats's early poems; sometimes associated with the equally symbolic cross, it generally symbolizes love, the heart's desire. In "The Secret Rose" it evokes the poet's Muse, guardian of ideal forms and in that respect the object of sacrifice and worship. The figure is properly ethereal, perfect in the sense which Yeats had in mind when he said that we love only the perfect and our dreams make all things perfect that we may love them. The rose is "far-off, most secret, and inviolate," its devotees "dwell beyond the stir / And tumult of defeated dreams." This country of the mind is Tirnanog, given mainly in rhythms shared with Rossetti. The rose is to "enfold" the poet, as she has already enfolded the Magi, Conchubar, Cuchulain and Fand, Caolte, Fergus, and a certain unnamed lover.

[18] *Mythologies*, p. 267.
[19] *Uncollected Prose*, p. 367.

The lover, hero of an Irish folk tale, mediates between the poet and the great mythological figures already celebrated, heroes in turn of action, passion, sorrow, and pride. These figures are true because people believe in them, immortal because that belief will never die, therefore ideal and essential but not abstract. So they are appropriately tended, enfolded by the rose. When the story of the human lover has been told, the poet says:

> I, too, await
> The hour of thy great wind of love and hate.
> When shall the stars be blown about the sky,
> Like the sparks blown out of a smithy, and die?
> Surely thine hour has come, thy great wind blows,
> Far-off, most secret, and inviolate Rose?

The wind of love and hate comes first from the Sidhe, then from the Enchanter in Shelley's "Ode to the West Wind," destroyer and preserver. It is hailed again in *The King's Threshold* when the poet says:

> Cry aloud
> That when we are driven out we come again
> Like a great wind that runs out of the waste
> To blow the tables flat. . . .[20]

The stars blown about the sky are seen in Blake's *Four Zoas*:

> And Man walks forth from midst of the fires: the evil is all consum'd.
> His eyes behold the Angelic spheres arising night & day;
> The stars consum'd like a lamp blown out, & in their stead, behold

[20] *Collected Plays*, p. 84.

> The Expanding Eyes of Man behold the depths of
>   wondrous worlds!
> One Earth, one sea beneath.[21]

The sparks and the smithy come from Cabalistic texts
and especially, as Allen Grossman has noted, from a
passage in von Rosenroth's *Kabbala Denudata*, translated by MacGregor Mathers, about the destruction of
prior worlds, worlds formed "without conformation."[22]
"Surely thine hour has come": the first of many induced
epiphanies in Yeats, here especially the hour when
three dreams cross—alchemy, symbolism, and poetry.
The poem expresses a poet's desire to transmute his
quotidian loves and sorrows "into some divine and
imperishable substance"; an ambition hardly more
miraculous than that of turning the youth at the breakfast table into a major Romantic poet. Success in these
enterprises would mean the creation of a new and
wondrous world.

The poem begins as if its chief object were to receive
Cuchulain and the other heroes into the Order of the
Golden Dawn: hence the hieratic tone, the movement
of figures as in a tapestry. The procession continues,
descending from gods to men, and Yeats develops
another part of the priestly role, prepares the next revelation: "I, too, await / The hour of thy great wind of
love and hate." The note of pride comes from Yeats's
association with the Rose, now invoked as the spirit of
poetry. Adept of the imagination in a heroic context, he

[21] William Blake, *Complete Writings*, ed. Geoffrey Keynes
(London, 1966), p. 379.
[22] Allen Grossman, *Poetic Knowledge in the Early Yeats, A
Study of "The Wind among the Reeds"* (Charlottesville, Va.,
1969), pp. 94–95.

is composing an Ode to the Poetical Character. The context is exalted, but it does not reduce the poet to shame or silence; he is a hero in his role if not in demonstrable achievement. I read the poem as an exemplary moment in Yeats's career because of the verve with which he declares himself member of a great company; that he carries it off can hardly be disputed. He has gained by pride of role what he could not have achieved by mere pride of station. Yeats is claiming kinship with the Muse on the basis of a great role accepted rather than a great work accomplished; he is a poet, different from the Muse only in degree. A Romantic poet who deals with such matters is bound to take them gravely, and it is well that he should; if the auspices are good, he gains, if nothing else, a new air of authority. Some poets deem themselves sufficient authority, but Yeats is of the other fellowship: of those poets who must join the visionary company and declare themselves in good standing with the Muse before they can gather their talents about them. Such poets need to become "the Poet" before they can do anything worthy. In many of his early verses Yeats moves in this direction, but "The Secret Rose" is the first occasion on which, by speaking to the Muse as a poet speaks to the spirit of poetry, he adds a new string to his Aeolian lyre. The string, which we recognize in the tone of pride, cannot be found by examining a certain bundle of accident and incoherence; it is a work of pure imagination.

The string is sounded again in "Adam's Curse," though the dominant tone is elegiac rather than proud. A poet who has loved his beloved for years and still loves her, but now hopelessly and knowing his hopelessness, speaks to her and her sister, "that beautiful mild woman, your close friend." The themes are love, beauty, and poetry, so we think of some Platonic academy and of fine discourse, except that the poet's conversation is poignant rather than speculative. The time is the end of summer; its emblems the waning moon, the shell of wisdom and prophecy; its rhythm a dying fall. The poem's structure embodies its feeling; beginning with forms, speeches, tokens of a brave start, but ending abruptly, when these poor things have failed and silence is all that remains. "In Memory of Major Robert Gregory" is a comparable occasion, so far as structure goes. If moral power is certified by speech, lapse into silence marks its loss and perhaps the poet's acceptance of that loss or his bewilderment in defeat.

Such poems do not merely come to an end. In "Adam's Curse" what is enacted in the first instance is the acceptance of defeat, the failure of a man's love, and then the failure of the entire terminology which that love sustained—in this case, the force of everything in life that Yeats praised as subjective and antithetical. For the moment, these powers have failed; they have been defeated by the primary world, objectivity, the tyranny of fact. Adam's curse: in Genesis God said to Adam, "cursed is the ground for thy sake, in toil shalt thou eat of it all the days of thy life." In the primary world it is the better part of prudence to bear the curse of Adam as genially as we can: the comforter gave this counsel in Yeats's beautiful poem, "The Folly of Being Comforted." "Adam's Curse" does not sponsor patience, but it moves to a condition in which the poor opposing spirit is worn out; the victory of time and objectivity is evidently complete. Meanwhile the conversation proceeds, setting up a rhetorical conflict between primary and antithetical terms. In beauty, the antithetical element is the beloved's "great nobleness," as Yeats described it in "The Folly of Being Comforted," "the fire that stirs about her, when she stirs." The equivalent in poetry is imagination, the inner fire, secret discipline. Poets and beautiful women are in league against "the noisy set / of bankers, schoolmasters, and clergymen / The martyrs call the world." But poets and beautiful women are subjective spirits, and for them the time is out of phase, they are faces belabored by time. In "No Second Troy" Maud Gonne's beauty is "a kind / That is not natural in an age like this, / Being high and solitary and most stern." As for imagination, it courts difficulty and is often defeated by its love: what is ruined, in "The Fascination of What's Difficult," is "spontaneous joy and natural content," and the imagination is compelled to "shiver under the lash, strain, sweat and jolt." The pain cannot be eased until Yeats defines a sense of experience that does not depend upon finalities of victory or defeat, and until he devises a corresponding idiom. The values that cry aloud in "Adam's Curse" are not assuaged until they are taken up in the different contexts of "A Prayer for My Daughter" and later poems. To be specific: these feelings are not released until the word "labour," epitome of Adam's curse, is transformed into the blossoming and dancing labor of "Among School Children."

But it is not enough to say that the poet in "Adam's Curse" accepts defeat or persuades himself to accept it; he does not hang his head. The poem is remarkable for the poise that it sustains between fact and value. If the world's verdict endorses fact, the reader is left in no doubt where value resides. Defeat is registered not as heroic or glorious, but as beautiful, the moral question is answered in aesthetic terms, and Yeats is a master of that resource. Poetry and love meet in the beautiful, which explains why of the three presences in the conversation Maud is contained in silence. Poet and friend have to make a case, but Maud's beauty is itself a declaration of independence. The poignancy of "Adam's Curse," especially when we read it with "The Secret Rose" not entirely forgotten, is that while in the earlier poem Yeats got whatever he needed from the symbols at hand and had merely to find his power in them, here the symbols cannot help, beyond providing an appropriate decor for his sorrow. Yeats's mastery in the later poem is a remarkable achievement of style, and its proof is composure, the dignity of tone with which time's cruelty is received. It is proper to speak of such poetry as a form of power, even where the official theme is the defeat of that power. The poet is not obliged to report that his values prevail, as a practical matter, in the objective world. In his first poems Yeats knew that he had this power, but he did not know what to do with it, beyond releasing it now in one way, now in another. His progress as a poet had to wait for the discovery that there was at least one way of converting divisions to poetic use, making chance amenable to that degree of choice.

The Play of Consciousness

● ●

11

There is a passage near the end of the second
book of *A Vision* where Yeats writes:

> My instructors identify consciousness with
> conflict, not with knowledge, substitute for
> subject and object and their attendant logic a
> struggle towards harmony, towards Unity of
> Being. Logical and emotional conflict alike
> lead towards a reality which is concrete,
> sensuous, bodily.[1]

It is my understanding that this sense of consciousness as conflict is the most important
article in Yeats's faith as a poet and that he
committed himself to it, at whatever cost, in the
first years of the new century. He may have felt
the need of it in his early relation with his
father—the need not to avoid or dissolve conflict

[1] *A Vision*, p. 214.

but to find value in conflict itself, the process rather than the end. If he could convert mere division, a pathetic fact of life, into conflict, a technique of poetic energy, he could take the harm out of the world's success and make an heroic drama even from the materials of ostensible failure. In *The Winding Stair* he writes of time, "We the great gazebo built," and of death, "Man has created death," because he is now skilled in the drama of consciousness and has no difficulty in converting fact to feeling. Without a flair for consciousness as conflict, he could not have done so. And while he speaks of "a struggle towards harmony, towards Unity of Being," the crucial part, I would maintain, is the struggle itself, rather than its end. The signal merit of the dramatic as a way of poetic life is that it allows its adept to retain his chaos; it is impartial in the employment of chaos as of order. Yeats's poetry does not give an impression of striving toward a single consummation; it does not make the reader think of an end to be reached, as he thinks of Eliot's poetry, for instance, striving to fulfill itself in *Little Gidding*, where earlier possibilities are worked out according to a logic of the imagination. Eliot's poetry is best understood by working back from its end, because the end was implicit in its logic from the very beginning. Yeats's poetry does not give this impression; it deploys itself in process, along the way of conflict; action incites reaction, statement calls forth counterstatement, each voice is given its due but a rival voice is always heard. No end to such a poetry is required, save that a man dies. The poetry is not defined by internal logic or by the positions reached, but by the reaching of positions; the act of struggle rather than the conclusion. The struggle is propelled by that energy which Yeats, recalling Blake's glowing use of the word, calls "excess." Excess is the degree of energy that turns pathos into passion, pity into pride: it converts passion to power.

So the first quality to remark in Yeats's mature work is that it takes conflict as a good, not as a necessary evil but as a subjective merit. Of his instructors he says again, "it was part of their purpose to affirm that all the gains of man come from conflict with the opposite of his true being."[2] Subjectivity and objectivity are "intersecting states struggling one against the other," and while Yeats has little good to say of objectivity in itself, its collaboration in conflict numbers it in the song, life being "impossible without strife."[3] The last phrase is not Yeats's weary recognition of a fact of life, but his assent to the principle of conflict; there is no pathos. A man's true being is determined, except that he is granted the freedom of defiance: conflict with his opposite is the definitive act of freedom. Poetry is the result of a "quarrel with ourselves,"[4] deliberately provoked and pursued. The fascination of what's difficult is not that it makes a problem but that it makes a drama: "Only the greatest obstacle that can be contemplated without despair rouses the will to full intensity."[5] The first poems of *In the Seven Woods* have the task of preventing despair, so that the will can persist, making conflict continuous. In *A Vision* Yeats says that Shelley "lacked the Vision of Evil, could not conceive of the world as a continual conflict, so, though great poet he certainly was, he was not of the greatest kind."[6] Whit-

[2] *Ibid.*, p. 13.
[3] *Ibid.*, pp. 71, 79.
[4] *Mythologies*, p. 331.
[5] *Autobiographies*, p. 195.
[6] *A Vision*, p. 144.

man and Emerson are touched with the same rebuke, though we may feel, incidentally, that Yeats is in no position to scold. His own vision of evil is extremely rarefied; he knows evil in one form only, the sadness with which a lover watches his beloved growing old. Evil is loss, loss of order, beauty, nobility. "Man is in love and loves what vanishes, / What more is there to say?"

Conflict, struggle, tension, and difficulty are terms of praise, then, because they are manifestations of the mind in its characteristic act. "Tension is but the vigour of the mind," Yeats wrote in a rejected stanza of "The Circus Animals' Desertion." The sentiment comes readily to him because, at least in his mature work, he loves to set his circus animals in conflict: Fergus and Conchubar, O'Connell and Parnell, Jupiter and Saturn, virgin and harlot, Rome and Greece, Russell and Whitehead. No force is rejected unless it is found too weak to engage with its opposite. The essential question is the definition of will. It is clear that Yeats's interpretation of Symbolism held back for several years his mature understanding of will and its relation to imagination. At the beginning he distinguishes sharply between them. Imagination takes a Symbolist form and is at home in trance, reverie, and its attendant rhythms; its matter is essence. Will is a busybody, rushing about the world, preoccupied with getting on. The distinction persists in Yeats's later work, but it is greatly modified, necessarily, because his theory of the Mask depends upon the validity of will; if the theory is to hold, will and imagination must conspire together, sinking their differences. But Yeats was slow in giving up the association of imagination with reverie, essence, and timelessness. There are moments even in his later poems when he slips back to the old dream. Still, the weight of evidence puts will and imagination in accord. In *A Vision* a man is classified according to the place of will in his diagram; will is sometimes called "choice," but by any name its milieu is "our inner world of desire and imagination," lunar and antithetical. "Personality," Yeats says, "no matter how habitual, is a constantly renewed choice."[7] At that stage the distinction between will and imagination is hardly material.

The theme is energy. In "The Death of Synge" Yeats declares that happiness "depends on the energy to assume the mask of some other self." All joyous or creative life is "a rebirth as something not oneself, something which has no memory and is created in a moment and perpetually renewed."[8] Yeats called this something an image, presumably because he wanted to keep it close to its source, the imagination, and because he wanted a word from the general vocabulary of vision: symbol might have done as well but for the fact that it bears a burden of personal and racial memories while image is in that respect free. A man's image may be chosen from another era, but it comes to the imagination free of circumstance. "Every passionate man," Yeats writes in "The Trembling of the Veil," "is linked with another age, historical or imaginary, where alone he finds images that rouse his energy."[9] But this merely tells a man where he ought to look for his opposite. We seek our opposite, and what we find is already related to us "as water with fire, a noise with silence."[10] We

[7] *Ibid.*, pp. 73, 84.
[8] *Autobiographies*, p. 503.
[9] *Ibid.*, p. 152.
[10] *Mythologies*, p. 332.

reject what comes too easily, because it is likely to be a gift from the primary world and, if so, it humiliates our imagination, defeats our energy. Joyous life is dynamic, it engages the whole man, we seek an image. Writing of Phase 15 in *A Vision* Yeats says that in that phase thought has become an image, inhabiting a world "where every beloved image has bodily form, and every bodily form is loved."[11] This indeed is the promised end, and a more forthright account of it than the general references to unity of being.

It is not a remarkable theory, nor does Yeats claim that it is original. Its elements come from the general understanding of Imagination in the Romantic tradition; Kant and Coleridge are its greatest exponents. Yeats has accepted the Romantic sense of imagination as a creative power, the finite counterpart, as Coleridge said in *Biographia Literaria*, of the original creative act of God; significantly, of the act by which God created himself, the divine *I Am*. Yeats's contribution to the theme is to translate it into theatrical terms; God becomes a great dramatist. The poet, in Yeats's version, becomes a great actor, taking unto himself a role directly opposite to his given nature. Living through that role, striking through the mask, the actor assumes a second nature, with this advantage over the first: that it is his own creation. The energy with which the actor commands his role is celebrated as style.

I am arguing that Yeats's cast of mind is best understood in theatrical terms. Theater brings everything together: consciousness as conflict, vigor of mind as tension, struggle, action, role, mask, will, gesture, speech, excess, form. Reading Yeats's greatest poems, we find them intensely dramatic; reading his most typi-

[11] *A Vision*, p. 136.

cal poems, when the exact dynamic balance is lost, we find them theatrical, and we wonder whether the term falls into much or little blame; if much, we say the poems are histrionic. In any event, theater is the art most congenial to his rhetoric and to his sense of life and form. When he draws upon the theme, he recurs to the same range of words: self-mastery, difficulty, discipline, the antithetical force, theater, style. As in "Estrangement," speaking of a relation between discipline and the theatrical sense:

> If we cannot imagine ourselves as different from what we are and assume that second self, we cannot impose a discipline upon ourselves, though we may accept one from others. Active virtue as distinguished from the passive acceptance of a current code is therefore theatrical, consciously dramatic, the wearing of a mask. It is the condition of arduous full life.[12]

In "The Death of Synge" he says that "the self-conquest of the writer who is not a man of action is style," and in "Estrangement" that "style, personality—deliberately adopted and therefore a mask—is the only escape from the hot-faced bargainers and the money-changers."[13]

The mind acts by conflict, sometimes accepting the opposition provided by the external world, but more often seeking its own antithetical image, constantly renewing its choice. The warriors include ideas of good and evil, solar and lunar values, symbol and history, self and soul, soul and body, Oedipus and Christ, Blake's Orc and Urizen, Yeats's Robartes and Aherne. Sometimes one side of a question will hold Yeats's

[12] *Autobiographies*, p. 469.
[13] *Ibid.*, pp. 516, 461.

affection for years, but sooner or later conflict begins again. Many of the early poems, for instance, are soul poems, high and rarefied, and after a while the daily world seems dissolved or refined out of existence, as if words scorned their earthly origin. The possession of a body, in such poems, seems an outrage. But Yeats cared for the contrary movement, too. In this phase he believes, and finds sanction in "the philosophy of Irish faery lore" for the belief, that "all power is from the body," so it is only a matter of time until that belief assaults the rhetoric of soul; a matter of time, and of the theatrical imagination. The poetry of body is inspired by Blake, and, I think, by Donne: "the body makes the minde," in Donne's version. In "Certain Noble Plays of Japan" Yeats says, "we only believe in those thoughts which have been conceived not in the brain but in the whole body"; and in *The Cutting of an Agate* he writes that "art bids us touch and taste and hear and see the world, and shrinks from what Blake calls mathematic form, from every abstract thing, from all that is of the brain only, from all that is not a fountain jetting from the entire hopes, memories, and sensations of the body."[14] Much later, in *On the Boiler*, he says that "our bodies are nearer to our coherence because nearer to the 'unconscious' than our thought,"[15] and thought is rebuked in the quarrel with action. In "Sailing to Byzantium" the body, like nature, is to be consumed, a dying animal. Yeats has not forgotten Dante and the "perfectly proportioned human body," but he is engaged in conflict with himself, and one force or the other must be in phase.

[14] *Essays and Introductions*, pp. 292–93.
[15] *Explorations*, pp. 446–47.

The organization of the *Collected Poems* is itself a kind of play; there is evidence that Yeats saw the dramatic possibilities and emphasized them. The *oeuvre* is understood as a sacred book, partly in deference to a motif in Mallarmé, but within that understanding each of the collections is a definite movement in a play; each is, to use his own phrasing, wrought about a vision, an attitude, a mood, a particular response to life which is dominant for the time being. The next book is the next moment, and it reflects a new and rival attitude, or the mind recoiling from its own creation. *The Tower* is improperly described as a development from everything that has preceded it; the idiom of development is misleading—it implies evolution. The relation between *The Tower* and the major books before and after, *Michael Robartes and the Dancer* and *The Winding Stair and Other Poems* is a dialectical relation, and we do well to think of the books as personalities in a play. The fact that, in retrospect, they form a pattern does not refute what has been said; their personalities are never blurred, the pattern is a theatrical form. When the play is over, conflicting characters are seen to have conspired with one another, in all ignorance; their formal relation is conspiracy, their immediate relation is conflict. Yeats writes poems, and then he makes them into books, not by merely collecting them but by choosing and arranging them to define a mood. The mood is never single-minded; it always contains the next source of conflict within its official program. There is always a Cuala Press in Yeats's imagination, not content with writing poems unless, from those poems, a beautifully harmonious book may be made. Then the books are ready to take part in the play.

It is possible to argue that Yeats's "consciousness as

conflict" is inspired, like nearly everything else, by Blake, recalling many relevant occasions in Blake, the readiest being *The Marriage of Heaven and Hell*, "Opposition is true Friendship," and again, "Without Contraries is no progression. Attraction and Repulsion, Reason and Energy, Love and Hate, are necessary to Human existence." But the ostensible kinship between Yeats and Blake, though asserted by Yeats and recited by his critics, is a questionable thing: it has been accepted largely because Yeats declared it a point of doctrine. Temperamentally, they were worlds apart, Blake hard, direct, assertive, while the Yeats who read him was a dreamer of lost times. In the early essays Yeats is enamored of Blake's poems, and his work with Edwin Ellis on Blake's texts is pious and often brilliant if not scholarly, but there is no real fellowship between the two poets. Yeats admired Blake's "precision," knowing that his own poems lacked that quality, and he hoped to gain it by the vigor of his admiration. Blake's influence on Yeats is found mainly in theory and desire, in the argument of his prose, in certain powerful images in the poems. But if we think of the character of the work itself, of Yeats's style as it governs the poems, we find little evidence of kinship. Blake gave Yeats many images, ideas, figures, and a prophetic ambition which was not the happiest gift; he did not give him what he needed, entry to the "theatre of the world." In fact, the influence of the entire neo-Platonic tradition upon Yeats, if we are thinking of genuine kinship, has been exaggerated. When Spenser writes in the "Hymn to Beauty":

What time this worlds great workmaister did cast
To make all things, such as we now behold,

It seemes that he before his eyes had plast
A goodly Paterne, to whose perfect mould
He fashioned them as comely as he could. . . .

we recognize the neo-Platonic tradition in the purity of
its central doctrine. But Yeats's poetry is not written
under that sign. What he received as neo-Platonism is
a loose anthology of occult images and figures available
to a poet who is avid for symbols. More accurately, his
anthology is largely Hermetic and Gnostic, it has more
to do with alchemical lore than with Plato or Plotinus.
But again the theatrical element is missing; what persists is a lexicon of associations and analogies. Plato's
may be "the truest poetry," as Edwin Muir said, but its
truth appealed to Yeats in one aspect only, the timeless,
the statuesque, the bronze repose. I do not argue that
this aspect is trivial: it is clearly related to its opposite,
and important for that reason, apart from other reasons.
But I shall argue later that the crucial figure in Yeats's
poetic life, if any single figure may be named, is
Nietzsche, and that the definition of Yeats's mind in
theatrical terms was achieved mainly under Nietzsche's
auspices, with some incitement from Heraclitus.

There is little point in saying that Yeats was a
philosophic poet, if we are strict in phrase. He was not,
like Wallace Stevens, a lover of ideas. Stevens found it
natural to think of ideas as works of art; never tempted
to live by ideas, he delighted to live among them. He
entertained ideas as forms of the beautiful; he was a
connoisseur and loved to contemplate his possessions.
Philosophy was to him a branch of aesthetics. An idea
touched him not in its truth but its formal perfection.
He envisaged "a poetry of ideas in which the particu-
lars of reality would be shadows among the poem's

disclosures,"[16] and he thought of the relation between light and shade as especially beautiful: thus he moved among ideas as he might stroll in a formal garden. Yeats was not on such easy terms with ideas; he distrusted philosophy as he distrusted any activity that relied so heavily on concepts. When he used the word "philosophy," as in "The Philosophy of Shelley's Poetry," or in several references to Balzac's philosophy, he meant certain patterns of imagery, the degree to which Shelley's domes, rivers, shells, and caverns make or appear to imply a consistent universe; certain liaisons of incident and symbol in Balzac. There is some evidence that Yeats was scandalized by secular philosophy, and that he wanted to define philosophy in its relation to images and not to ideas or concepts; images being closer than ideas or concepts to the religious sense of life. Mircea Eliade has argued that the rise of experimental science in the seventeenth century was possible only because substances had begun to lose their sacred attributes: the difference between chemistry and alchemy is not that one is true and the other a delusion but that alchemy offered itself as a sacred act, and chemistry came into its own when substances had lost their sacred attributes.[17] Nostalgia is a sufficient explanation for the fact that alchemy has never been destroyed by chemistry: alchemists are those who remember an ancient rite. Philosophy in Yeats's unofficial sense, endorsed by his version of Symbolism and the *anima mundi*, enabled him to think of the world as

[16] Wallace Stevens, *Opus Posthumous* (New York, 1957), p. 187.
[17] Mircea Eliade, *The Forge and the Crucible*, trans. Stephen Corrin (London, 1962), p. 9.

sacred—like Swedenborg's "desolate places," animated by spirits. He did not always wish to do so; his relation to natural forms was not invariably a religious service. But in this phase the only philosophers he needed were those who restored to the natural world its sacred and animate character.

The great enemy was Locke. Yeats read him in the Romantic way of Blake and Coleridge, and resented, as they did, Locke's separation of the primary and the secondary qualities of matter. It is still a disputed point how sharp the separation in Locke really is, but Yeats took the Romantic reading for granted. In this account the primary qualities are inseparable from the external body, and they are independent of the mind of the perceiver: the paraphrase of Locke is rough, but it must serve a turn. Secondary qualities are the sensations as of color, sound, taste, and so forth, produced in the perceiver's mind by the primary qualities. There are no innate ideas. Yeats interpreted Locke as offering an insidious abstraction: "and from that day to this," he wrote, "the conception of a physical world without colour, sound, taste, tangibility, though indicted by Berkeley as Burke was to indict Warren Hastings fifty years later, and proved mere abstract extension, a mere category of the mind, has remained the assumption of science, the groundwork of every text-book." It was only a short step, then, to "that form of the new realist philosophy which thinks that the secondary and primary qualities alike are independent of consciousness."[18] Two fears are active in Yeats at this point, the fear of abstraction, and the fear that substances cannot retain their sacred character if in their own right they retain only the primary qualities, solidity, extension,

[18] *Essays and Introductions*, pp. 400–401, 405–406.

figure, mobility, and number. So he distinguished, in the poem "At Algeciras," between the actual shells he gathered on the beach at Rosses Point and "such as are in Newton's metaphor." The passage in Newton reads:

> I do not know how I may appear to the world; but to myself I seem to have been only like a boy, playing on the seashore, and diverting myself, in now and then finding another pebble or prettier shell than ordinary, while the great ocean of truth lay all un-discovered before me.[19]

Presumably Yeats was outraged by talk of an ocean of truth distinct from the personally certified truth of the shells; so Newton and Locke denied spirit to "the world's body." Even an erotic poet would be outraged. In a letter to T. Sturge Moore Yeats argued that "nothing can exist that is not in the mind as 'an element of experience,'" and he maintained that this stance would "liberate us from all manner of abstraction and create at once a joyous artistic life."[20] He did not pursue the question, however, and he was relieved to find that Whitehead agreed with Berkeley and a poet was free to agree with both.

Berkeley took up Locke's challenge. "By Matter, therefore," he wrote in the *Essay of the Principles of Human Knowledge*, paraphrasing Locke, "we are to understand an inert, senseless substance, in which extension, figure, and motion do actually subsist."[21] As Yeats wrote in the Diary of 1930, "Descartes, Locke, and

[19] David Brewster, *Memoirs . . . of Sir Isaac Newton* (1885), II, 407. Quoted in A. N. Jeffares, *A Commentary on the Collected Poems of W. B. Yeats*, p. 350.
[20] Ursula Bridge, ed., *W. B. Yeats and T. Sturge Moore: Their Correspondence* (London, 1953), p. 69.
[21] Berkeley, *Works*, eds. A. A. Luce and T. E. Jessop, II (ed. Jessop; London, 1949), 44–45.

Newton took away the world and gave us its excrement instead. Berkeley restored the world. . . . Berkeley has brought back to us the world that only exists because it shines and sounds. A child, smothering its laughter because the elders are standing round, has opened once more the great box of toys."[22] Berkeley established and liberated the imagination by denying material substance independent of perception: he was right, as the child is right. Yeats associated Berkeley with the irrefutable truth of a child gathering shells at Rosses Point, and he loved the philosopher for that memory. Substance could be felt again as sacred, though it was a difficult point whether its sacred character was innate, a function of its divine origin, or derivative, a function of its relation to man. To Yeats, it was enough for holiness if a thing was related to man; on this point he parted from Berkeley. The philosopher, Yeats complained, "deliberately refused to define personality, and dared not say that Man in so far as he is himself, in so far as he is a personality, reflects the whole act of God."[23] The division between Berkeley's God and man is absolute. Yeats wanted to assimilate God to man, and he was led to do so because Blake had already gone to that point in his annotations on Berkeley's *Siris*: "God is Man & exists in us & we in him." That is: God is the human imagination. In one of the captions to *There Is No Natural Religion* Blake rejects Locke and runs beyond Berkeley: "Man's perceptions," he declares, "are not bounded by organs of perception; he perceives more than sense (tho' ever so acute) can discover."[24] Berkeley restored to the poet his box of toys and the

22 *Explorations*, p. 325.
23 *Essays and Introductions*, p. 408.
24 William Blake, *Complete Writings*, ed. Geoffrey Keynes (London, 1966), p. 97.

imagination to play with them, though he did not allow him to believe that a generous God might in that play be domesticated. Blake led Yeats to believe that the play, imaginative vision of the world, was holy, though Blake did not ascribe any special value to the toys, save as baubles for children to play with. Yeats wanted to believe, for the most part, that box and play were sacred, and that man was divine to the degree of his creative joy. He could then write poems like those "Supernatural Songs" in which Ribh rebukes Saint Patrick:

> Natural and supernatural with the self-same ring
> are wed.
> As man, as beast, as an ephemeral fly begets, God-
> head begets Godhead,
> For things below are copies, the Great Smaragdine
> Tablet said.

To revert to Locke and Berkeley: much of the argument can be summarized as a gloss upon one of Yeats's cryptic "Fragments":

> Locke sank into a swoon;
> The Garden died;
> God took the spinning-jenny
> Out of his side.

Yeats included these lines in the Introduction to *The Words upon the Window-Pane*, prefaced by the following:

I can see in a sort of nightmare vision the 'primary qualities' torn from the side of Locke, Johnson's ponderous body bent above the letter to Lord Chesterfield, some obscure person somewhere inventing the spinning-jenny, upon his face that look of benevolence kept by painters and engravers, from the middle of the eighteenth century to the time of the Prince Consort.[25]

There is also an earlier observation in the same Introduction, where Yeats says that in Swift's time Unity of Being was still possible though somewhat overrationalized and abstract, more diagram than body. In the Diary of 1930 this is described again as a "sinking into abstraction," partly shown by Berkeley's failure to triumph over Locke. In the essay on Berkeley Yeats recurs to Locke's abstraction: "It worked," he says, "and the mechanical inventions of the next age, its symbols that seemed its confirmation, worked even better." "Only where the mind partakes of a pure activity," he insists, "can art or life attain swiftness, volume, unity": he is thinking of Coleridge's remark that Shakespeare drew the Nurse in *Romeo and Juliet* from direct observation, passive sense impression, but Hamlet, the Court, the whole work of art, out of himself in a pure indivisible act.[26]

The tone of the argument is rueful. In the "Fragment" it is sharpened—one apprehension set against another, a drama rather than a lament. The poem enacts the defeat of Berkeley and Blake by Locke's abstraction. Locke sank into the swoon of abstraction, more diagram than body. Marshall McLuhan argues in *The Gutenberg Galaxy* that "the Lockean swoon was the hypnotic trance induced by stepping up the visual component in experience until it filled the field of attention. At such a moment the garden (the interplay of

[25] *Explorations*, pp. 358–59.
[26] *Essays and Introductions*, pp. 401, 409–10.

all the senses in haptic harmony) dies."[27] The justification of this gloss is an elaborate argument, not yet
settled one way or the other, to the effect that the
printing press reduced the several modes of perception
to one, the other senses being, as it were, anaesthetized.
Blake supports the argument, castigating Bacon, Newton, and Locke for their "single vision." The single
vision is the "point of view," where the observer is
trapped before the observed scene, experience is con-
gealed, restricted to those items which the observer sees
from his fixed position; he might as well be deaf and
dumb. The God of the Industrial Revolution took
Locke's primary qualities out of his side, thereby insur-
ing that man would always be alone among machines:
the parody of the creation of Eve goes at least as far as
that; God made her lest Adam be alone. The effect of
Locke's swoon and Newton's sleep is the loss of that
entire world of experience for which the appropriate
metaphors are organic, vegetal, bodily, nuptial.

But the relation of poetry and philosophy is seriously
incomplete, so far as Yeats is concerned, if it is con-
ducted solely in terms of realism versus idealism. If it
begins and ends with a choice, Yeats's position is clear:
idealist. Cassirer's statement of the idealist case is satis-
factory: idealists want to transform "the passive world
of mere *impressions*, in which the spirit seems at first
imprisoned, into a world that is pure *expression* of the
human spirit."[28] Yeats was content with that: there
are moments in which his imagination seems predatory

[27] Marshall McLuhan, *The Gutenberg Galaxy: The Making
of Typographic Man* (London, 1962), p. 17.
[28] Ernst Cassirer, *The Philosophy of Symbolic Forms*, trans.
Ralph Manheim (New Haven, 1953), I, 81.

in its idealist fervor, and we resent the demands made upon the innocent objects of his attention, as the swan becomes "another emblem there!"; there are other moments in which the box of toys is enjoyed for its plenitude, the imagination revels in its fortune, the strict question of epistemology is evaded. But there is a point beyond which further consideration of subject and object is null, and we feel that the English philosophers have not given Yeats the idiom he needs.

In September 1902 John Quinn sent Yeats his own copy of *Thus Spake Zarathustra* and impersonal copies of *The Case of Wagner* and *The Genealogy of Morals*. For months thereafter Yeats seems to have read virtually nothing but Nietzsche. Apologizing to Lady Gregory for tardiness in correspondence, he said, "The truth is you have a rival in Nietzsche, that strong enchanter. I have read him so much that I have made my eyes bad again. . . . Nietzsche completes Blake and has the same roots—I have not read anything with so much excitement since I got to love Morris's stories which have the same curious astringent joy."[29] Yeats's letters to George Russell and to Quinn over the next few months show that his reading in Nietzsche made him dissatisfied with the work he had done in *Ideas of Good and Evil*, which had recently appeared. "The book is too lyrical, too full of aspirations after remote things, too full of desires," he told Quinn. To Russell he explained, "The close of the last century was full of a strange desire to get out of form, to get to some kind of disembodied beauty, and now it seems to me the contrary impulse has come. I feel about me and in me an

[29] *Letters*, p. 379. The letter is dated "? Sept. 26, 1902," in this edition, but it now appears that the correct date is later, between December 27, 1902, and January 3, 1903.

impulse to create form, to carry the realization of beauty as far as possible." These conflicting movements of the soul, as Yeats called them, the desire to transcend forms and the desire to create forms, he associated with Nietzsche's Dionysiac and "Apollonic" movements, as he called them. "I think I have to some extent got weary of that wild God Dionysus, and I am hoping that the Far-Darter will come in his place."[30] He told Florence Farr that he was trying "to lay hands upon some dynamic and substantialising force as distinguished from the eastern quiescent and supersensualizing state of the soul—a movement downwards upon life, not upwards out of life." I would maintain that Yeats's "consciousness as conflict" began to define itself in this excited reading of Nietzsche, when he found himself turning from one mood to its opposite and sought some means of retaining both. In *The Will to Power* Nietzsche writes:

> Handel, Leibniz, Goethe, Bismarck—characteristic of the *strong* German type. Existing blithely among antithesis, full of that supple strength that guards against convictions and doctrines by employing one against the other and reserving freedom for itself.[31]

In the *Autobiographies* Yeats mentions that not one of his contemporaries had "a talent for conviction": it is apparent that Nietzsche's philosophy of risk was precisely what Yeats needed to enable him to live with passion in that state. "Live dangerously," Nietzsche says in *The Gay Science*, "Build your cities under Vesuvius." The will to power "can manifest itself only

[30] *Ibid.*, p. 403.
[31] Friedrich Nietzsche, *The Will to Power*, trans. Walter Kaufmann and R. J. Hollingdale (London, 1968), No. 884, p. 471.

against resistances; therefore it seeks that which resists it." Later: "It is not the satisfaction of the will that causes pleasure . . . but rather the will's forward thrust and again and again becoming master over that which stands in its way." The feeling of pleasure, Nietzsche continues, "lies precisely in the dissatisfaction of the will, in the fact that the will is never satisfied unless it has opponents and resistances." The happy man is "a herd ideal."[32]

It is also at least probable that Nietzsche's attack upon the pretentions of spirit, as opposed to the wonderful fact of body, helped to dislodge Yeats from the Innisfree of his early poems: the admission of body and the dynamic relation between body and soul are crucial in Yeats's artistic life, since body involves time, place, and history in its power. Ultimately, the aesthetic of combat that Yeats endorsed is based upon facts of biological life, upon the energy required for the survival of an organism. One of the purposes of games in an industrial society is to divert the combative instincts, which otherwise break out in violence; the procedure has only one defect—that it fails in its grand design while succeeding on minor occasions. Its value is aesthetic. One of the distinctive qualities of Yeats's imagination is that it revels in combat, cultivates force at the risk of aggression and power at the risk of violence, lest the organism die of sloth and satisfaction.

To Yeats, Nietzsche was in these respects the archetypal Hero, exemplar of Phase 12 in *A Vision*. "True to phase," Yeats writes, "he is a cup that remembers but its own fullness." There is now, he continues, "the greatest possible belief in all values created by

[32] *Ibid.*, No. 656, p. 346; No. 696, p. 376.

personality." Yeats speaks of "a noble extravagance, an overflowing fountain of personal life . . . a philosophy which is the logical expression of a mind alone with the object of its desire." Finally, "the man follows an Image, created or chosen by the Creative Mind from what Fate offers; would persecute and dominate it."[33] Recall Nietzsche's description of "the great man":

> He knows he is incommunicable: he finds it tasteless to be familiar; and when one thinks of it, he usually is not. When not speaking to himself he wears a mask. He rather lies than tells the truth; it requires more spirit and will. There is a solitude within him that is inaccessible to praise or blame, his own justice that is beyond appeal.[34]

The doctrine of the Mask is more fully developed in *Beyond Good and Evil*, but already it is clear that the image which Yeats sought is more Blake than Plato, more Nietzsche than Blake.

Yeats's copies of Nietzsche are heavily annotated. When something appealed to him he underlined it, often adding several comments in the margin. An underlined passage in *Beyond Good and Evil* occurs where Nietzsche is declaring the differences between a master morality and a slave morality. Speaking of the Master as the creator of values, Nietzsche refers to "the feeling of plenitude, of power which seeks to overflow, the happiness of high tension, the consciousness of riches which would fain give and bestow; the noble man also helps the unfortunate not (or scarcely) out of sympathy, but rather out of an impulse produced by the superabundance of power." In the third section of

---

[33] *A Vision*, pp. 127–29.
[34] Nietzsche, *op. cit.*, No. 962, p. 505.

Zarathustra's Prologue, where Zarathustra says that, God being dead, the worst sin is to blaspheme against the earth, or to rate supernatural life higher than the meaning of the earth, Yeats writes in the margin: "Yet the 'supernatural life' may be but the soul of the earth out of which man leaps again, when the circle is complete." Yeats is already converting Nietzsche into cyclic, gyring terms—reincarnation being one of the few beliefs Yeats really held, his small talent for conviction fulfilled there if rarely elsewhere.

His relation to the strong enchanter is based upon the needs of a particular moment, but it became a definitive relation and was never abandoned or even greatly modified. Specifically, the kinship depends upon Nietzsche's terminology of power, the endorsement of will and conflict, his feeling for the theatrical principle, his sense of tragedy, contempt for the herd, glorification of the hero—"One should recall what one owes to Napoleon: almost all the higher hopes of this century—"; his feeling of power working from within, his "curious astringent joy." Neitzsche's criticism of Darwinism is that life is not the adaptation of inner to outer circumstances, but will to power, which incorporates and subdues more and more of what is "external." The Christian ideal is contemptible because it proposes as the universal standard of value the virtues by which happiness is possible for the lowliest: it grossly flatters the instinct for preservation in the least vital of all classes. The herd is justifiable merely as a means of preserving the species.

That these sentiments appealed to Yeats can hardly be disputed; their impact is felt in poems, plays, essays, where the Nietzschean gesture may be registered throughout Yeats's later work. One factor is especially important, the concept of the hero. Yeats needed such a concept to justify his hierarchical sense of life, his belief that life is defined by its imperious moments, great deeds, and by these alone, society valued for its masters. The hero is an antithetical fiction; his idiom is power, will; his sense of life dynamic, theatrical. In *The King's Threshold* Seanchan says:

> The stars had come so near me that I caught
> Their singing. It was praise of that great race
> That would be haughty, mirthful, and white-bodied,
> With a high head, and open hand, and how,
> Laughing, it would take the mastery of the world.

and later, just before his death:

> I need no help.
> He needs no help that joy has lifted up
> Like some miraculous beast out of Ezekiel. . . .
> Dead faces laugh.[35]

This is pure Nietzsche, the simultaneous presence of joy, triumph, and death, the hero laughing into the face of death. The gesture came from Nietzsche, and Yeats received it as if he had spent his life waiting for it, as in a measure he had. Certainly, many of Yeats's motives would have gone without definition but for Nietzsche: the proof is in the plays, especially in *The King's Threshold* and Congal's death scene in *The Herne's Egg*; in the poems "Upon a Dying Lady," "The Gyres," "Lapis Lazuli," and many more. The Nietzschean gesture in the face of death is the personal version of the "laughing, ecstatic destruction" in the historical myth of "The Second Coming."

Yeats linked Nietzsche with Blake but not, so far as

[35] *Collected Plays*, pp. 89, 93.

I have found, with Heraclitus. This is surprising, not only because Nietzsche's admiration of Heraclitus is explicit in *Twilight of the Idols* and other books, or because Heraclitus is a model for Zarathustra, type of the lonely hero; but because both philosophers offer, in effect, escape from subject and object. In Heraclitus, as in Nietzsche, energy displaces knowledge as "the good," action replaces concept. It is not known how much of Heraclitus Yeats read, and it may be that his study was even more fragmentary than Heraclitus's texts. Only one phrase stayed in his mind, but it is significant. At the end of *The Resurrection* the Greek cries:

> O Athens, Alexandria, Rome, something has come to destroy you. The heart of a phantom is beating. Man has begun to die. Your words are clear at last, O Heraclitus. God and man die each other's life, live each other's death.[36]

Heraclitus's words (Fragment 66 in some modern editions) are quoted several times in Yeats—at least four times, which is certainly too often, in *A Vision* and twice in *On the Boiler*—and a strong echo is heard in "Byzantium." Yeats does not quote the phrases to endorse the survival of the soul after the body's death, though such a purpose would be justified; invariably, he recalls the fragment when his theme is the death of one force and its vicarious life as its opposite: "an age is the reversal of an age." Normally, Yeats suppresses "God and man" in favor of "opposites," and the forces in question may be Rome and Byzantium, Discord and Concord in "The Great Wheel," solar and lunar periods in "The Completed Symbol," Lazarus and the Good

---

[36] *Ibid.*, pp. 372–73. See Peter Ure, *Yeats the Playwright*, p. 113.

Samaritan. In each case the opposites depend upon the energy that holds them together, the "high tension" of their relation. What is common to Heraclitus and Nietzsche is the declared complicity of opposites. Nietzsche was more useful than Heraclitus because he offered Yeats a theater of personality, and the gestures appropriate to tragic joy. Strangely, Yeats associated him with Balzac. In a lordly conversation with Hugh Kingsmill in 1924 Yeats announced, "All Nietzsche is in Balzac," the theme on that occasion being Balzac's "romanticization of power."[37]

Nietzsche's impact on the poems is demonstrable: words of power are used with a special intonation as if they were pre-empted for an imperial theme. In many cases, words find their meanings driven beyond good and evil. It is difficult to use such words as "arrogant" and "bloody" in the twentieth century with eulogy in mind, but a Nietzschean rhetoric succeeds where the dictionaries fail:

> Blessed be this place,
> More blessed still this tower;
> A bloody, arrogant power
> Rose out of the race
> Uttering, mastering it,
> Rose like these walls from these
> Storm-beaten cottages— . . .

Most of the work is done by "rose," which makes good and evil irrelevant in the rhetoric of power; "uttering, mastering it" justifies the Norman conquerors according to master morality. If any sentimental feelings persist, they are driven away by "storm-beaten"; the Normans

[37] Michael Holroyd, ed., *The Best of Hugh Kingsmill* (London, 1970), pp. 273–76.

are now a force of nature. The effect is made easier by recalling a passage in *Per Amica Silentia Lunae*:

> There are two realities, the terrestrial and the condition of fire. All power is from the terrestrial condition, for there all opposites meet and there only is the extreme of choice possible, full freedom. And there the heterogeneous is, and evil, for evil is the strain one upon another of opposites; but in the condition of fire is all music and all rest.[38]

But the gloss is hardly necessary. In the poem itself, "Blood and the Moon," power as distinct from wisdom is, "Like everything that has the stain of blood, / A property of the living," and in the immediately preceding poem, "A Dialogue of Self and Soul," the condition of blessedness follows when one has cast out remorse. Norman conquerors are justified because they were masters; their relation to Celtic natives is that of tower to storm-beaten cottage; "blessed" has become, under this pressure, a secular word. The transition from "uttering" to "mastering" is so swift that we hardly register the ethical leap we make from one to the other; the tone of hauteur is enough. Yeats learned from Nietzsche how to maintain this tone even when the context is violent: the equivalent in Nietzsche is the rhetoric of fire and ascent, a procedure studied by Gaston Bachelard in *L'Air et les Songes*—"*Le feu n'est qu'un trait qui monte.*" The ethical question soon appears archaic. A context is prepared that excludes ethics; words that enter now are slanted toward a Nietzschean "transvaluation of values." A word in such a context becomes a new word.

The Nietzschean note is heard most clearly, perhaps

[38] *Mythologies*, pp. 356–57.

too clearly, in the third section of "Vacillation," in "Parnell's Funeral," "Lapis Lazuli," "An Acre of Grass," and pervadingly in the last poems and plays. Nietzsche propelled Yeats toward the idiom of combat, theater, unity of opposites. He is certainly responsible for some of the ensuing rant as well as the splendor: he conspired with Yeats in bravado. But Yeats's greatest poems depend upon the theatrical sense, and it is difficult to regret an association which helped him to write with such eloquence.

"Sailing to Byzantium" is a case in point: it is a dialogue of self and soul, except that "dialogue" makes the relation sound explicit. Rather, the relation is a matter of gestures, feelings, leanings toward one limit rather than another. The poem begins with an old man looking toward death; looking back, too, at the young world of love, credences of summer held as if they were eternal, the "sensual music" of youth. The man at the breakfast table feels his age and thinks of death, but the poet, old in his own way, imagines death as immortality, one of the great human limits, trying to take the sting out of it. The poem is a ritual to transform death, representing it as immortality, not by denying the fact but by creating it, transforming it, turning it into subjective purpose. The first stanza is full of the honey of generation, and even if the old man intervenes to say that generation is also death, the flow of summer feeling continues. The second stanza accepts, for the moment, the rift of body and soul:

> An aged man is but a paltry thing,
> A tattered coat upon a stick, unless
> Soul clap its hands and sing, and louder sing
> For every tatter in its mortal dress.

The scarecrow is brought to life; this is the force of "unless," preparing the magic. The god of life is the soul, seen as a Blakean child, visionary of innocence. "Soul clap its hands and sing," as if to answer the lovers in the first stanza with a corresponding joy; even though the joy is largely what the poet learns from the lovers. There is, so far as feeling goes, no contradiction. The old man is changed into a poet and he knows his place; it is not on earth, in nature, but in the eternity of art. It makes little difference to the poem whether we feel Byzantium as an island of the blessed, a land of eternal youth, or the holy city of Romantic art, so long as we receive from it suggestions of permanence, perfection, and form. "God's holy fire" is not likely to mean more than immortality registered as a continuous imaginative act, the fire that makes all simple. The poet is asking to be received into that order, to be made over again as child and seer. For such a boon he is ready to "die" to summer: "consume my heart away." The body is felt, now more than ever, as a "dying animal." In the last stanza, like Keats saying, "Already with thee!" Yeats yearns for the freedom of Byzantium:

> Once out of nature I shall never take
> My bodily form from any natural thing,
> But such a form as Grecian goldsmiths make
> Of hammered gold and gold enamelling
> To keep a drowsy Emperor awake;
> Or set upon a golden bough to sing
> To lords and ladies of Byzantium
> Of what is past, or passing, or to come.

The determination with which the profession of faith is made testifies to the depth from which the feeling comes; there can be no doubt of the strain. Casting the body aside, the poet turns to new analogies with the desperate certainty of a recent convert. But these golden figures are still the old, human roles, translated into emblems of art. The resolved soul is to occupy itself, like any poet or storyteller, keeping drowsy emperors awake or singing, like any bird in a tree, to lords and ladies. The themes are themes of time, "what is past, or passing, or to come," and differ only in their setting, though that difference is great.

But the direction of feeling in the poem is not as determined as its scenario implies, and if the last line restores the poet to the cycle of generation, it marks an essential qualification in the entire movement of feeling. The poet speaks of the "artifice" of eternity, and some readers take the reference as strongly ironic; but it is not. "Gather me . . ." means gather me into a self-subsistent world, an artifice indeed but only in the sense that it is man's creation and, Yeats would hold, all the nobler for that. A slight feeling of distance is certainly present in the word, but not as much as, say, in the reference to "monuments of unageing intellect" in the first stanza. The last line of the poem, too, is stronger evidence; the difficulty encountered in moving out of nature is greater than the scenario promised. Yeats's feeling, in this respect like language itself, is still half in love with the old fleshpots—time, place, memory, history. This is in the nature of words. Music is the Symbolist art because its relation to the empirical element is weak; it finds no difficulty in releasing itself to a condition of pure form. But words drag the ball and chain behind them, the burden of time. T. Sturge Moore complained to Yeats that "Sailing to Byzantium," "magnificent as the first three stanzas are, lets me down in the fourth, as such a goldsmith's bird is as much nature as a man's body, especially if it only sings like Homer and Shakespeare of what is past or passing or to come to Lords and Ladies."[39] Yeats thought the point well taken, and wrote "Byzantium" as if to answer it. In fact, "Sailing to Byzantium" is preserved by its helplessness, by the conflict between its official feelings, and by Yeats's reluctance to resolve the conflict except by continuing it. It is a sign of the integrity of the poem that, responsive to rival feelings, it registers their strain, one upon the other. The poem is saved by Yeats's scruple and by his theatrical flair.

Before reading "Byzantium" we should advert to a passage from Yeats's Diary of 1930:

> I am always, in all I do, driven to a moment which is the realisation of myself as unique and free, or to a moment which is the surrender to God of all that I am. . . . Could those two impulses, one as much a part of truth as the other, be reconciled, or if one or the other could prevail, all life would cease. . . . Surely if either circuit, that which carries us into man or that which carries us into God, were reality, the generation had long since found its term.[40]

The two circuits are really self and soul, one "as much a part of truth as the other." "Byzantium" begins as if everything Yeats meant by self or heart were already transcended, consumed in the simplifying fire. But the critical question to ask of the first stanza concerns the poet's attitude to the apparent victory of soul over the fury and the mire of human veins. There is nothing here to correspond to the heartfelt evocation of love

[39] Bridge, *op. cit.*, p. 162.
[40] *Explorations*, pp. 305, 307.

and summer in the first lines of "Sailing to Byzantium," a hint that Yeats's dominant feeling has moved toward the proffered forms of transcendence: there is an impression that transcendence has been achieved too easily; the difficulties have not been allowed to assert themselves. These difficulties are recognized in the winding and unwinding of the bobbin in the second stanza, but the figure does not register any remarkable degree of vitality; we do not feel the strain between two allegiances. The last lines of the stanza make a dangerously vatic moment in the rhetoric of the poem. Much depends upon the reception of the Heraclitean motif, "death-in-life and life-in-death"; it is hardly clear, unless we associate it with the sentence already quoted from Yeats's marginalia on Nietzsche, that the supernatural life "may be but the soul of the earth out of which man leaps again, when the circle is complete." "I hail the superhuman": the mage in Byzantium is calling the generic soul of man, coming from the *anima mundi* and returning to it. "Shade more than man, more image than a shade": presumably to mark the indeterminate status of the spirit, the séance has just begun. This indeterminateness is echoed again in the third stanza, "more miracle than bird or handiwork," but the line can hardly do more than attach an aura to the singing bird of "Sailing to Byzantium." The artificial bird can crow like the cocks of Hades, heralds of rebirth on Roman tombstones, or it can disdain the mere "complexities of mire or blood"; the bird is close to the scornful dome of the first stanza. In the next stanza the "blood-begotten spirits" die in Byzantine flames; they are carried on the dolphin's back like the Holy Innocents going to Heaven in Raphael's statue:

> Astraddle on the dolphin's mire and blood,
> Spirit after spirit! The smithies break the flood,
> The golden smithies of the Emperor!
> Marbles of the dancing floor
> Break bitter furies of complexity,
> Those images that yet
> Fresh images beget,
> That dolphin-torn, that gong-tormented sea.

The question here again is the recognition of self and soul, each as much a part of truth as the other, and the answer chiefly depends upon the force of "break" in this stanza. Does it conspire with the flames and the marbles in reducing the poor multiplicity of life to unity, or does it resist, in life's behalf? Does the language insure "reality and justice in a single thought" by showing a tragic drama on that dancing floor? It seems to me that the bitter furies of complexity have done what they can, but they cannot do enough, there is not enough here to give that "complexity" convincing force. The word is used as if it referred to something already certified; but nothing has been certified, certainly not enough. That the images are self-creative, like the flames, is something, so we rush into the last line with reality and justice not quite established. That line is magnificent in a good cause. "Dolphin-torn" now has the force of human action behind it, and the "gong-tormented sea" is a cry from time and earth. Mostly the feeling comes in the rhythm, which is entirely different from the hieratic tone of the mage. These are now, at the last moment but not too late, the accents of passion turned upon loss: it is the nature of the poem, after all, that it resolves nothing. To Yeats, as to Stevens, "the imperfect is our Paradise," and it may be our Hell, too.

It is customary nowadays to read "Byzantium" as a parable of the poetic imagination, putting it in the company of similar parables from Coleridge to Stevens; taking the blood-begotten spirits as the poor human feelings, broken but also forged by the creative imagination and refined to the "glory of changeless metal." Life is sacrificed for art, and Romantic feeling urges that a world is well lost in such a grand cause. Read in this way, the poem seems to me a small thing. I should wish to have it more literally, as more in keeping with Nietzsche's voice in the background. The plot of the poem is given in the first stanza of "Vacillation" on the next page in the *Collected Poems*:

> A brand, or flaming breath,
> Comes to destroy
> All those antinomies
> Of day and night . . .

But there is the same problem here of gauging the full significance of "destroy": its first associations are exalted, in keeping with Yeats's cult of fire and flame. But then:

> The body calls it death,
> The heart remorse.
> But if these be right
> What is joy?

Body and heart cannot be expected to welcome the flame; remorse is the violence that conscience does upon the heart, death is violence only greater in degree. What is joy? What is the source of that joy which is active even in destruction, like Nietzsche's tragic joy? The answer is given in the fourth section of the poem. So the weight of "destroy" must be held in suspense; we cannot take the full strain of its meaning until the poem is complete. This applies also to "break" in "Byzantium"; it waits upon the complete action.

A word about the poem and its "circuits." The first stanza is all Soul; the rhetoric favors the second circuit, "that which carries us into God." The crime of death and birth has not been forgotten, but it trails out from the second circuit and barely survives the second stanza; its survival depends upon the extent to which such heart words as "mire," "fury," and "complexities" assert themselves against their rivals. The second and third stanzas hail the superhuman: the changeless metal is not that of Sato's ancient blade, emblem of history and tradition in the "Dialogue of Self and Soul"; it is assimilated to the moonlit dome and declares a like scorn. But at least the mire and blood are recalled, if only to be refined and simplified, antinomies of day and night to be destroyed by the flames, "flames that no faggot feeds," since this is the second circuit, the Way of the Soul. The triumph of Soul would be complete but for the dolphin, friend to man and Self. As the dolphin carries the souls to Paradise, the reality of the first circuit breaks in: the poet looks back at the waves of poor reality breaking upon the marbles of the floor. The first circuit, "that which carries us into man," moves the reader into the cycle of nature, honey of generation, mire and blood and time.

The mind is its own theater. One of the effects of "consciousness as conflict" in Yeats is that conventional terminologies, including standard ethical values, are often displaced: energy assumes the right to displace them. The basis of Yeats's consciousness is energy; conflict is the plot of energy. It would be neat to say that Yeats thinks of energy as the internal power that corresponds to the vital power in nature. Personal energy would then appear a pious acknowledgment of energy at large, its spirit in keeping with God as absolute energy. But in Yeats the direction is nearly reversed. The first energy he recognizes is within, and his theories and motifs are designed to extend that recognition, hopefully to present All in consonance with the irrefutable One. Thus he tends to derive a sense of the vital spirit at work in the world from the certainty of a vital spirit at work within himself (the problem is to accommodate the world to himself). So also he tends to judge an act in relation to the energy it concentrates; the more the better. Heroes are heroic because their degree of energy is high; timid people are miserable in Yeats's eyes because their degree is low. Finally, the gap between knowledge and action is closed, imperatively, because action subsumes knowledge; the Platonist scholar in his lonely tower lives not for contemplation but for power, that purely internal power which is energy. Conflict is valued because, one energy confronting its opposite, the mere person is transformed.

History and the Secret Discipline

III

We should consider now the sources of that energy. In "The Symbolism of Poetry" Yeats says that "all sounds, all colours, all forms, either because of their preordained energies or because of long association, evoke indefinable and yet precise emotions, or, as I prefer to think, call down among us certain disembodied powers, whose footsteps over our hearts we call emotions."[1] A reader may prefer to think that the last phrases are blarney, but Yeats meant them almost literally, and it is difficult to understand his version of Symbolism unless we take the words strictly. In "The Philosophy of Shelley's Poetry" he speaks of the Great Memory as "a dwelling-house of symbols, of images that are living souls."[2] The aura we feel in a symbol is

[1] *Essays and Introductions*, pp. 156–57.
[2] *Ibid.*, p. 79.

the presence of the supernatural in the natural; the souls of the dead are understood as living in places which are sacred because of that residence, as in mountains "along whose sides the peasant still sees enchanted fires."[3] Yeats's evidence is not an elaborate theory of the occult; it is the fact that certain images, certain places, have been long "steeped in emotion." In the essay on magic he writes that "whatever the passions of men have gathered about becomes a symbol in the Great Memory, and in the hands of him who has the secret it is a worker of wonders, a caller-up of angels or of devils."[4] It follows that Yeats distinguished even more sharply than other writers between symbolism and allegory. A symbol is "the only possible expression of some invisible essence, a transparent lamp about a spiritual flame; while allegory is one of many possible representations of an embodied thing, or familiar principle, and belongs to fancy and not to imagination: the one is revelation, the other an amusement."[5] Symbol redeems fact, because through symbol the imagination enters experience, as Christ redeemed fact in the Incarnation (a comparison made, incidentally, in the commentary on Blake by Yeats and Ellis). Belief in reincarnation is endorsed by assent to tradition; Symbolism is the hermeneutics of that faith.

I have argued that the first stirrings in Yeats are a feeling of his own latent power, certified by energy, and that his relation to nature is derived from within; if so, his theory of Symbolism is not an attempt to make sense of the world, but to define the world in his own image. We may let that argument stand. But Yeats

[3] *Ibid.*, p. 114.
[4] *Ibid.*, p. 50.
[5] *Ibid.*, p. 116.

proposed to find in the theory not only plenitude and power but discipline. "It is only by ancient symbols, by symbols that have numberless meanings besides the one or two the writer lays an emphasis upon, or the half-score he knows of, that any highly subjective art can escape from the barrenness and shallowness of a too conscious arrangement, into the abundance and depth of Nature."[6] I take this to mean that symbols mediate between the individual consciousness, which would otherwise be solipsist, and the given world, which would otherwise be alien. Symbols partake of the created and the given; they are given, but given by creative souls not unlike our own. A race is a communion of souls: a poet who writes in these terms must be, in Yeats's sense, a Symbolist. "The poet of essences and pure ideas must seek in the half-lights that glimmer from symbol to symbol as if to the ends of the earth, all that the epic and dramatic poet finds of mystery and shadow in the accidental circumstances of life."[7] Here is one escape from solipsism, the more reliable because it is consistent with the liaison of poetry, tradition, and symbolism. The poet's art is devoted to essence; he fills our minds "with the essences of things, and not with things"; his chief instrument is rhythm, which keeps us "in that state of perhaps real trance, in which the mind liberated from the pressure of the will is unfolded in symbols."[8] This is Yeats's early idiom, taken largely from Pater and Symons—"in art rhythm is everything," Symons wrote in 1898—and he tired of it, or turned to its opposite, but he always associated symbolism, rhythm, and trance. It may be, he said, that the arts

[6] *Ibid.*, p. 87.
[7] *Ibid.*, p. 87.
[8] *Ibid.*, p. 159.

"are founded on the life beyond the world, and that they must cry in the ears of our penury until the world has been consumed and become a vision."[9] A Symbolist disciplines himself by scruple.

With Yeats in mind, therefore, it is well to understand Symbolism as the literary form of magic, except that what the mage does consciously the poet does half consciously and half by instinct. The ancient secret is common to both disciplines. When someone asked Yeats, of his belief in magic, "It is just a game, isn't it?" Yeats answered, "One has had a vision; one wants to have another, that is all."[10] The answer is irrefutable, unless one is in a position to deny the first vision. A mage believes he can do what a Symbolist does, but deliberately. The activities are so congenial, one to the other, that their double presence in the minds of "the tragic generation" is entirely natural: two forms of the same impulse, to command a spiritual power without incurring the commitment of an objective church. Cornelius Agrippa's *De Occulta Philosophia* was one of Yeats's sacred books, and *Prometheus Unbound* was another: their joint presence in his mind is neither an indulgence nor an aberration, but a choice. Magic was congenial to Yeats for many reasons, but especially because it depended upon the imperative power of language, Rimbaud's *alchimie du verbe*. When Yeats writes, as in the plays, "I call to the eye of the mind," he is not devising a pretentious way of saying, "Let us think of . . ." The phrase issues from his feeling for the common grammar of mage and poet. Cassirer has written that "all word-magic and name-magic are based on the assumption that the world of things and the world

[9] *Ibid.*, p. 184.
[10] *Autobiographies*, pp. 298–99.

of names form a single undifferentiated chain of causality and hence a single reality."[11] This goes some way to account for the incantatory note in Yeats's style, where his sentences are more readily understandable if we take them as rituals, prescriptions, interdictions than as secular utterances. In the background we sense the presence not merely of hermetic procedures but of Mallarmé's *"mystère d'un nom."* Reality is invoked through the natural power common to poet and mage, the power described in Durkheim's *The Elementary Forms of the Religious Life* and other books. The religious life is not always explicable in relation to power, but when Yeats described himself as "very religious" he meant it as a phrase of power; in that sense, a religion is what a man creates, not a creed that he values because it is independent of his hands.

Symbols are of all kinds, as Yeats writes, "for everything in heaven or earth has its association, momentous or trivial, in the Great Memory, and one never knows what forgotten events may have plunged it, like the toadstool and the ragweed, into the great passions."[12] Continuity of passion is the test. Continuity of power is proof, to Yeats, that souls do not die: "The dead living in their memories are, I am persuaded, the source of all that we call instinct, and it is their love and their desire, all unknowing, that make us drive beyond our reason, or in defiance of our interest it may be."[13] The *anima mundi*, "described by Platonic philosophers and more especially in modern times by Henry More,"

[11] Ernst Cassirer, *The Philosophy of Symbolic Forms*, trans. Ralph Manheim (New Haven, 1953), I, 118.
[12] *Essays and Introductions*, p. 50.
[13] *Mythologies*, p. 359.

is more than a storehouse of images and symbols, since its content is what a race dreams, whatever it remembers; its memories and dreams remain active, and often assume a palpable form. The great soul may be evoked by symbols, which are the script of images italicized by the supernatural, but the spirits are not mere functions of ourselves, they have their own personalities, they make sport and mischief. Perhaps the best interpretation of the *anima mundi* is that it is the subjective equivalent of history, a nation's life in symbols; it is not our invention, but it may respond to our call.

Yeats did not distinguish very sharply between image and symbol. He accepted the meaning of image mainly from Boehme and William Law—"Image meaneth not only a creaturely resemblance, in which sense man is said to be the Image of God; but it signifieth also a spiritual substance, a birth or effect of a will, wrought in and by a spiritual being or power." Imagination is then "the power of raising and forming such images or substances, and the greatest power in nature."[14] Image and symbol differ, apparently, only in degree. In the symbol, much of the spiritual work has already been done, and it requires only natural sensitivity and a little imaginative power to disclose the symbol's force. Yeats found in Blake's *Milton* a figure to represent the process by which symbols are received:

> When on the highest lift of his light pinions he arrives
> At that bright Gate, another Lark meets him & back to back
> They touch their pinions, tip tip, and each descend

[14] Quoted in *Uncollected Prose*, p. 400.

To their respective Earths & there all night consult
  with Angels
Of Providence & with the Eyes of God all night in
  slumbers
Inspired, & at the dawn of day send out another
  Lark
Into another Heaven to carry news upon his
  wings.[15]

Yeats interpreted the passage as meaning that man
attains spiritual influence in like fashion: "He must go
on perfecting earthly power and perception until they
are so subtilised that divine power and divine perception descend to meet them, and the song of earth and
the song of heaven mingle together."[16] He did not
associate it with a similar passage in *The Revolt of
Islam* about "Spring's messengers descending from the
skies," though a section from the same Canto VII
represented for him the subjective action which he
describes in "Ego Dominus Tuus." Shelley's Cythna
speaks of the inner power that enabled her to transform
the world. Either we are darkened by the shades, she
says, or we "cast a lustre on them." Then she continues:

My mind became the book through which I grew
  Wise in all human wisdom, and its cave,
Which like a mine I rifled through and through,
  To me the keeping of its secrets gave—
  One mind, the type of all, the moveless wave
Whose calm reflects all moving things that are,
  Necessity, and love, and life, the grave,
And sympathy, fountains of hope and fear;

[15] William Blake, *Complete Writings*, ed. Geoffrey Keynes
(London, 1966), p. 526.
[16] *Uncollected Prose*, p. 394.

Justice, and truth, and time, and the world's natural
sphere.[17]

Shelley made the imprisoned Cythna, as Yeats says,
paraphrasing the next stanza, "become wise in all
human wisdom through the contemplation of her own
mind, and write out this wisdom upon the sands in
'signs' that were 'clear, elemental shapes, whose small-
est change' made 'a subtler language within language',
and were 'the key of truths which once were dimly
taught in old Crotona.' "[18] So "Ille" in "Ego Dominus
Tuus" seeks an image, and calls to his opposite for the
disclosure of "all that I seek." But if one mind is to be
"the type of all," it must be suffused in symbols, else
contemplation becomes an arid exercise.

In the idealist tradition the contemplation of one's
own mind is bound to be the exemplary act, like
Mallarmé watching himself in a mirror in order to
think. One's own mind is the place of incarnation. In
Yeats, contemplation—not "slippered Contemplation"
but a dynamic act—registers the mind as moving within
its own circle, confronting its opposite, gathering its
energy into a symbolic gesture. Dance is its embodiment. The subtler language within a language corresponds to the self-appeasing gestures of the dancer, a
sensual metaphysic within the physical body. The
classic emblem is Mallarmé's Hérodiade, who gathers
everything into the artifice of the dance:

> *Et tout, autour de moi, vit dans l'idolâtrie*
> *D'un miroir qui reflète en son calme dormant*
> *Hérodiade au clair regard de diamant . . .*[19]

---

[17] Shelley, *Poetical Works* (London, 1970), p. 113.
[18] *Essays and Introductions*, p. 78.
[19] Stéphane Mallarmé, *Oeuvres Complètes* (Pléiade ed.; Paris,
1945), pp. 41–49.

or in Symons's translation, which Yeats quotes in "The Tragic Generation":

> And all about me lives but in mine own
> Image, the idolatrous mirror of my pride,
> Mirroring this Herodiade diamond-eyed.

Mallarmé's virgin is crucial in the mythology of Yeats's dance plays and especially his Salomé play, *A Full Moon in March*: it may even be fancied that the dance plays were designed to complete what Mallarmé left unfinished in the drama of "Hérodiade." In "The Tragic Generation," after the quotation from Symons's translation, Yeats says, "Yet I am certain that there was something in myself compelling me to attempt creation of an art as separate from everything heterogeneous and casual, from all character and circumstance, as some Herodiade of our theatre, dancing seemingly alone in her narrow moving luminous circle."[20] We have here an almost complete aesthetic for a Symbolist theater; the dancer, a dynamic image, moves by her own sweet will and in the climax of the play disengages herself completely from character and circumstance, the stage a luminous circle answering to her mind, everything transfigured in the energy of the dance. Yeats described it again in *A Vision*, the perfection of subjectivity in Phase 15:

> The being has selected, moulded and remoulded, narrowed its circle of living, been more and more the artist, grown more and more "distinguished" in all preference. Now contemplation and desire, united into one, inhabit a world where every beloved image has bodily form, and every bodily form is loved.[21]

[20] *Autobiographies*, p. 321.
[21] *A Vision*, pp. 135–36.

Yeats has moved rather surreptitiously from Mallarmé to Dante. I would maintain that the admission of body and bodily motives qualifies the otherwise pure Symbolism of this theater. For the moment it is enough if we recognize that Yeats's Symbolism, which owes much to Shelley, is turned toward the theater by Mallarmé. Mallarmé's theater is not the same as Nietzsche's, and the Noh theater differs in important respects from each, but for the present Mallarmé is enough, Symbolism being our theme. The celebrated program outlined in "*Crise de Vers*" establishes the contours of Symbolism, so far as we need them in reading Yeats. Mallarmé has been describing the new motive, "*pour ne garder de rien que la suggestion* " (to keep nothing but the suggestion), and he continues, "*Instituer une relation entre les images exacte, et que s'en détache un tiers aspect fusible et clair présenté à la divination.*[22] (To institute an exact relationship between the images, and let there stand out from it a third aspect, bright and easily absorbed, offered to divination.) The chief characteristic of a Symbolist poem, in this context, is that the third aspect disables interpretation or criticism except in so far as these responses aspire to divination: the images, since they live by action rather than by knowledge, refuse to be translated. This gives them their esoteric aura. The climax of a dance play does not disclose a meaning separable from the aura of this action; it is exactly the form which subjective intensity takes, and apart from that form it is nothing. As for the words, it would be better if we received them as "vocables" than as counters to be construed from a diction-

---

[22] Mallarmé, *op. cit.*, p. 365. (Translation by Anthony Hartley. See his *Mallarmé* [London, 1965], p. 169.)

ary. The equivalent act in Yeats's poetry is "In Memory of Major Robert Gregory," where "the entire combustible world" is consumed in a moment, fire returning to its origin in fire. "Flare" brings Pater, Nietzsche, and Mallarmé together, but the poem shows how Yeats transcends his origins with an entirely personal rhythm.

The elegy is also Yeats's incandescent tribute to the antithetical life. It has recently been impugned on the ground that Robert Gregory was not the remarkable man Yeats took him to be, but this argument is sordid. The men celebrated in the poem are presented not as major figures but as companions of Yeats's life, vivid people in their own right. The text may be glossed from *Autobiographies* and *A Vision*, but the gloss is unnecessary. The people described are not all lonely or subjective types (Synge's subjective lives, for instance, being over, as Yeats says in the *Autobiographies*). But the several people lead to Robert Gregory: his life-in-death, death-in-life disengages itself, like the Symbolist dancer, from accident and multiplicity, even from the generous variety acknowledged in Lionel Johnson, Synge, and George Pollexfen. The climax is prefigured by the "measureless consummation" of which Johnson dreamed. The rhetoric implies that Gregory, "our perfect man" and exemplar of Unity of Being, achieved that illumination by the intensity of his antithetical power:

> We dreamed that a great painter had been born
> To cold Clare rock and Galway rock and thorn,
> To that stern colour and that delicate line
> That are our secret discipline
> Wherein the gazing heart doubles her might.

The secret discipline is that contemplation of one's own mind which Yeats admired in Shelley's Cythna; he gives another version of it in "A Bronze Head":

> Propinquity had brought
> Imagination to that pitch where it casts out
> All that is not itself. . . .

If a reader asks why the landscape of Clare and Galway is necessary, the answer is: antithetical imaginations need an obstacle and, if an obstacle is not given, devise one. The imagination in this phase fulfills its energy by casting out all that is not itself; but it needs something to cast out. Even Hérodiade acknowledged "*et tout, autour de moi*" as *materia poetica* to be gathered into the image. "The gazing heart doubles her might" by committing herself to her proper discipline. The artist sees not with the eye but with the mind's eye: the Symbolist acts by exclusion, narrowing the luminous circle for greater concentration and intensity. At this point the imagination is indeed the will, electing to make the world anew in its own image. The effort is an internal act.

"Gazing" is a strict term for Yeats, and depends upon a distinction between two, or perhaps three, modes of vision. In "Dove or Swan," near the end of *A Vision*, Yeats describes the period of Roman decay, distinguishing between the qualities of Roman and Greek statuary for evidence. Roman vision is rendered in the glance, which is characteristic of a civilization in its last phase; it is the sign of administration, measurement, the civil service, character rather than personality, the gap between subject and object, inert bodies "as conventional as the metaphors in a leading article." These eyes are subjectively dead, while objectively they have taken and are about to lose possession of the world. Yeats contrasts this glance with the gaze: the gaze is purely internal and secret, "vague Grecian eyes gazing at nothing, Byzantine eyes of drilled ivory staring upon a vision, and those eyelids of China and of India, those veiled or half-veiled eyes weary of world and vision alike."[23] The distinction between these last attitudes, if it exists, need not concern us here. The gaze is the subjective act of the Grecian figure, described also as dance, gazing at nothing, or presumably at its own antithetical nature and the correspondingly challenged antinomies. Greek statues are also Symbolist poems. Yeats's words make a sequence, culminating in the Oriental equivalent of the "flare."

The gaze is internal and secret, it issues in the self-begotten dance, in "heroic reverie"—a phrase from "A Bronze Head"—and even, however ruefully this was to appear, in the enchanting "dream" of "The Circus Animals' Desertion." Any idiom, if held against resistance, is bound to win or appear to win, because nothing can defeat its logic. That Yeats hoped to find all in the symbol is not a scandal but proof that aesthetic systems are irresistible; a system can be defeated by another system only if the second is self-consistent and the first is not. A well-wrought fiction is irresistible. Yeats could certainly have found everything in the symbol by allowing his dancer to take possession of the world, converting it to an image. But he was not, after all, a thoroughgoing Symbolist. Even in the elegy on Robert Gregory he allowed his system to be bewildered, brought to silence by brute fact, by "the abrupt indis-

[23] *A Vision*, pp. 276–77.

cretion of events," as Symons said on another occasion. In the last stanza, after the conflagration, Yeats comes down to the daily world and finds it relentless. In other poems man may have invented death, but now death, like the bitter wind "that shakes the shutter," scorns horsemen, scholars, soldiers, antithetical poets, secret disciplines. Yeats's imagination tries to provide "a fitter welcome" for his guests than the bitter wind, "but a thought / Of that late death took all my heart for speech." The dance is broken. Yeats's sense of fact and his sense of justice admit the rival terminology, however rude. The admission undermines his security as Symbolist, but it gives with one hand what it took away with the other; it allows him, by entertaining conflict, to find a more inclusive and a greater art. "Life is the last thing he has learnt," Symons wrote of Yeats in 1904 with an implication that the lesson was now well established in his art.[24] In his mature poems Yeats does not allow his sense of life to be overwhelmed by the charm of a system, even one of his own devising: he became a major poet when he determined to live by that creed.

Some readers deny that Yeats achieved such an art. Ezra Pound, who admired Yeats's work, rebuked him for the excess of his Symbolism. In Canto 83, with Yeats in view as well as Baudelaire, Pound insists that "*Le Paradis n'est pas artificiel*"; the reference is to Baudelaire's *Les Paradis artificiels*, an ode to the hieroglyphics of dream and symbol. Paradise is not *artificiel*, Pound says, repeating a warning already given in Cantos 74, 76, and 77. Paradise exists, finite and historical, if "only in fragments," such as excellent

[24] Arthur Symons, *Studies in Verse and Prose* (London, n.d.), p. 231.

sausage, the smell of mint, and Ladro the night cat. Pound teases Yeats:

> And Uncle William dawdling around Notre Dame
> in search of whatever
> paused to admire the symbol
> with Notre Dame standing inside it.[25]

The point is well taken, so far as it refers to Yeats's tendency to replace the given world by a figment of the Symbolist imagination, "in search of whatever," since this effect is possible only by vacancy, taking one's eye off the object. Pound is insisting that the given world, such as it is to a common imagination, is more durable than the bronzes of Symbolism: it stands forth, bodied against the golden bird and the hieroglyphic dream of "Byzantium."

There is a relevant passage in the "Esthétique du Mal" where Stevens writes movingly of such matters:

> How cold the vacancy
> When the phantoms are gone and the shaken realist
> First sees reality. . . .

A few stanzas later, Stevens speaks of one who is alone in both the peopled and the unpeopled worlds:

> In both, he is
> Alone. But in the peopled world, there is,
> Besides the people, his knowledge of them. In
> The unpeopled, there is his knowledge of himself.
> Which is more desperate in the moments when
> The will demands that what he thinks be true?[26]

[25] *The Cantos of Ezra Pound* (London, 1954), p. 563.
[26] Wallace Stevens, *Collected Poems* (New York, 1954), pp. 320, 323.

I quote these passages from Pound and Stevens to mark a transitional stage in the argument: from Pound, to concede that a point has been made against Yeats, and then to say that it is merely a point and does not reflect the full situation; from Stevens, to say that Yeats, in love with phantoms as he was, still faced the desperate moments in which "the will demands that what he thinks be true." It is wrong to present Yeats merely as Mallarmé's ephebe or a slightly more robust Symons; I have perhaps already gone too far in that direction. Only a small fraction of Yeats's poetry sounds as if it were written under the auspices of *"L'après-midi d'un faune."* There are moments in which he is satisfied with whatever the subjective will chooses to do, but there are other moments in which he is satisfied with nothing less than the truth, conceived as independent of his will. These rival allegiances are brought together by the theatrical force of his imagination, and there is reason to think that his poetry was preserved by his scruple.

Against symbol, therefore, we should place history, meaning whatever the imagination recognizes as distinct from itself. History in this sense means not only the past but the usual, whatever comes from the nature of things and not from the imagination; in "A Dialogue of Self and Soul" Yeats called it "life." We may concede that Yeats was sullen with history understood in this spirit, since his first love was symbol: "the cracked tune that Chronos sings" was peculiarly harsh to his ear. He allowed history to enforce itself only because it was the strongest rival to symbol and therefore a constructive obstacle: it could not be denied, and might in some moods be welcomed. In a letter to Dorothy Wellesley

(May 4, 1937) Yeats said that Mallarmé "escapes from history," but "you and I are in history," specifying, however, that he meant "the history of the mind." Roger Fry's translation of Mallarmé "shows me the road I and others of my time went for certain furlongs. . . . It is not the road I go now, but one of the legitimate roads."[27] But we must be careful with the word. We speak of the past, but we do not bind ourselves to say whether what we speak of is boldly independent of ourselves or is one of our attendant slaves. History is a predicate, hopefully to be reconciled to the subject, but it is not the subject's minion. It is common nowadays to speak of history as if it were a pure fiction, and at that point we confuse history with historiography, the past with our book of the past. In the *Eighteenth Brumaire*, however, Marx said that men make their own history, but they make it under circumstances directly encountered, given, transmitted from the past: the tradition of the dead generations, he said, weighs like a nightmare on the brain of the living. It may be said of Yeats that from one nightmare he made another, different from the first only because its monstrous lineaments were the products of will; *A Vision* is proof. But the evidence runs both ways, and Yeats never freed himself from double allegiance. He respected the past as different from himself, one more version of an irreducible reality, but he longed to feel that the past was his oyster. He accepted the past as given, but given to satisfy his need. Like other historians, amateur and professional, he found in the past whatever his sense of form required. One of the purposes of *A Vision* is to declare the susceptibility of time

[27] *Letters on Poetry from W. B. Yeats to Dorothy Wellesley* (London, 1940), p. 135.

and history to a tragic pattern, Nietzschean in tone: the past becomes a "memory theatre," apocalyptic in its climax. If the book is considered eccentric, it cannot be for this reason; it is no more willful than other grandiose histories by Lamprecht or Burckhardt. Like these, Yeats's book ties historical events to its chariot; the emperor declares the victory of his fiction. The poems are greater than *A Vision* because they force the fictive element to encounter certain moments, richly imagined, in the cycle of time. "The Magi," for instance, fits the pattern of history outlined in *A Vision*, but it also testifies to a perennial feeling, for which no gloss is required. Yeats may be right or wrong about the next historical gyre, but success or failure in prediction makes no difference to the power of "The Gyres," which is certified by an inveterate feeling and by that alone.

The official pattern of history is an apocalypse, life felt in terms of a violent limit, the next turn of the gyre. Historical periods as given in the diagram at the beginning of Book 5 of *A Vision* are correlated to the twenty-eight phases of the moon, Yeats's Great Year. Recurrence is the law, whether we think of it benignly as cycle, "eternal return," or harshly as gyre or vortex. Nietzsche's Zarathustra celebrates recurrence as the wedding ring of rings— "Oh, how should I not lust for eternity and for the wedding ring of rings—the Ring of Recurrence!"—but Yeats's idiom conspires with the violent figures of his imagination as if they alone issued from the Spirit of History. "The world begins to long for the arbitrary and accidental, for the grotesque, the repulsive and the terrible, that it may be cured of desire,"[28] he writes near the end of *A Vision* as if to cure himself of desire, now that he has had his life. Ages are

[28] *A Vision*, p. 295.

described in a grand sweep, A.D. I to A.D. 1050 disposed in twelve pages, like Lamprecht treating the history of Germany from 500 B.C. to A.D. 1904 in an hour's lecture. I suppose the justification is that the historian can trace a pattern without noting every point in it.

Smaller-scale maps are available in Yeats's occasional essays. In the essay on Spenser, for instance, he maintains that Spenser's death in 1599 marked the end of "the Anglo-French nation," sometimes called Merry England, the old feudal nation which had been established when the Normans made French the language of court and marketplace. Elizabethan poetry coincides with a quarrel to the death between the old Anglo-French civilization and the new Anglo-Saxon values arising amid Puritan sermons and Marprelate tracts. "This nation had driven out the language of its conquerors," Yeats says, "and now it was to overthrow their beautiful haughty imagination and their manners, full of abandon and wilfulness, and to set in their stead earnestness and logic and the timidity and reserve of a counting-house." "Anglo-French Chaucer" is the great figure of the merry time, while Langland and Bunyan conspire with the Puritan nation. In Bunyan, "religion had denied the sacredness of an earth that commerce was about to corrupt and ravish"; but "when Spenser lived the earth had still its sheltering sacredness." Spenser was by nature "altogether a man of that old Catholic feudal nation, but, like Sidney, he wanted to justify himself to his new masters"; so he curbed the wild creatures of his imagination in deference to forms of allegory which were the products of a merchant culture. But "he had been made a poet by what he had almost learnt to call his sins."[29]

[29] *Essays and Introductions*, pp. 365 ff.

The essay on Spenser resumes in some detail a moment in history; after the Fall, it rehearses the joys of medieval unity. Yeats never wrote a *Mont-Saint-Michel and Chartres*, but like Henry Adams he implied an Eden in history, where body was not bruised to pleasure soul. That he found this felicity in the period from Chaucer to Spenser hardly matters; his historical sense is governed by his aesthetic sense, his sense of form, particularly tragic form. So it demanded an Eden in time, from which man ejected himself. In that Eden hero and peasant lived with the same excess, intensity signifying unity of being, unity of culture, experience brought to the pitch of form. The earth was sacred, and the souls of the dead inhabited desolate places. The only enemy was a Satan who turned his eyes toward money and machines, splitting thought and feeling, consciousness and experience. Now that mechanical force is about to become supreme—the year is 1925—the hero's only portion is defiance. Frenzy is forcing the next play onto the stage. Passion is the energy of recurrence: "for passion desires its own recurrence more than any event."[30] The understanding of history requires, like *A Vision*, applied typology. The historical sense, Nietzsche's sixth sense, is racial memory.

It follows that Yeats valued the past as the stuff of poetry and drama; he made of history a dramatic poem, a long poem. The events themselves are fated, but what we make of them is free, with such freedom as can be wrested from fate. What makes such a poetry endlessly possible is the correspondence of mind and world, certified by symbols: this enables the poet to bear with the fact that a mind is only as rich as the images it con-

[30] *Mythologies*, p. 354.

tains. Yeats's mind was peopled by images drawn from mythology and history: he did not take dictation from those images, but turned them to theatrical purpose, setting them astir. He was not a mere parcel of memories. The mythology most congenial to him was Celtic, with some additions from Indian lore. The history most congenial to him was that of Renaissance Italy, mainly illustrated in the history of art, and with some important additions from the history of Ireland in the eighteenth century, Berkeley, Swift, Goldsmith, "the people of Burke and of Grattan."

There was also, most bitterly, the history of his own time. I emphasize this last to make the point that, beginning with *In the Seven Woods*, Yeats's poetry admits into the otherwise self-enclosed garden of art the lives of other people—rarely ordinary people, I concede, but sufficiently common to acknowledge a reality that cannot be dissolved. These "presences" are palpable, and they correspond to the vernacular idiom of the poems they inhabit. The result is that the professed Symbolist is often, in practice, hardly a Symbolist at all: the student of Mallarmé resorts to Jonson and Donne. Style in these poems is a testament to values still persisting in the finite world, and it encourages Yeats to mediate between his rival dreams, Innisfree and apocalypse. In *The Wild Swans at Coole*, especially, he reaches a dynamic accommodation with history, which allows him to retain the old persuasions of idealism and subjectivity while acknowledging the sturdy independence of other people. With that acknowledgement comes the irreducible reality of fact, body, and time. *The Wild Swans at Coole* is vivid with a life that Yeats is willing to concede he has not invented: a short list of its manifestations includes George Pollexfen, Synge, Lionel Johnson, Iseult Gonne, Robert Gregory, "the living beauty" as distinct from "dazzling marble," the fisherman, "the form / Where the mountain hare has lain," Mabel Beardsley, Maud Gonne. These indisputable figures are set in league with other figures from mythology and Yeats's fiction: the Sphinx, the Buddha, Robartes, Aherne, the Fool, the Hunchback, Diarmuid and Grainne. What is common to both lists is the affection they stir, and this is proof enough. The book is perhaps misleadingly named, because it refers to birds which have offered themselves too readily, at least since Shelley's *Alastor*, for symbolic purposes—"A swan there was, / Beside a sluggish stream among the reeds." Yeats's reference to Coole qualifies the offer, tying it to history, but hardly with enough force, because the great house was already transcending history to become an emblem. Still, the balance is beautifully held in the poems themselves. *The Wild Swans at Coole* is history, consistent with Symbolism; *The Tower* is Symbolism, glancing ruefully at history. The balance is always difficult in Yeats, because it is foreign to his nature to delight in a world he has not made. The price an idealist art pays for its self-delighting power is a certain fretful note when the auspices are wrong, when the brute world insists on breaking in or the internal power fails and magic drifts away. It is remarkable that Yeats's middle poems transcend, to such a degree, their official aesthetic: nothing but moral power, to the degree of genius, can account for it. He was made a great poet by what he had almost learned to call his weakness—a weakness for reality.

"Among School Children" is the poem to read, if it

comes to a choice, to see how vivid the tension between history and symbol can be, and how satisfying. A prior condition, or at least an essential quality in the actual engagement of the two, is that each is given a fair chance. It is usual to interpret the first stanza in a more ironic spirit than I would favor, mainly because readers expect Yeats to use the word "modern" as a term of distaste, but on this occasion, by my reading, he does not. The schoolroom activities described in this stanza are charming, and only a gruff reading takes them as anything else:

> The children learn to cipher and to sing,
> To study reading-books and histories,
> To cut and sew, be neat in everything
> In the best modern way. . . .

There is external evidence that Yeats was pleased with this Montessori school[31] and praised it for being exceptional, indeed of remarkable cultivation. But the evidence is hardly necessary. "Cipher" is enough to show, by its archaic quality, that this is a grammar school of courtesies. The irony in the "sixty-year old smiling public man" is turned upon himself, not upon the school, the nun, or the children.

In the second stanza Yeats, as if recalling the heartsick note on which "Adam's Curse" had ended, recites an occasion on which the lover and his queen were in tune, "our two natures blent / Into a sphere," the first motif of unity in a poem that ends with two resplendent figures flowering in the same cause. I shall not go through the several stanzas; it is enough that we catch

[31] Donald Torchiana, "'Among School Children' and the Education of the Irish Spirit," in Jeffares and Cross, eds., *In Excited Reverie*, pp. 123–50.

the reverberations set astir in the contrasts: between childhood and age, nuns and mothers, the body in flower and the body in decay, Adam's curse diversely laid upon beautiful women and comely youths, the pain of mothers, sons, and lovers, the woman as "a living child" and as a "Ledaen body," daughter of the swan. In the seventh stanza Yeats distinguishes between images, eternal objects of our passion:

> Both nuns and mothers worship images,
> But those the candles light are not as those
> That animate a mother's reveries,
> But keep a marble or a bronze repose.
> And yet they too break hearts. . . .

It is my impression that these lines make the structural figure of the entire poem. Two sets of images are juxtaposed, and the difference between them is great, but at the end they converge, sharing one quality. The relation is not a simple contrast, because much of Yeats's feeling, as the poems of Byzantium and "All Souls Night" testify, yearns toward "a marble or a bronze repose." The images that "animate a mother's reveries" are irrefutable, so there is no question of the contest being decided on a simple verdict. Common to both sets is the power to break hearts. The antinomies are not destroyed but resolved; the poet makes peace, retaining both, justifying both by the passion they incite. The two sets are joined as one, both being eternal, invoked now as "Presences," Yeats's translation of "images" into persons. These presences, being eternal, are "self-born mockers of man's enterprise," and the effort of the last stanza is to send a lark aloft, hoping to meet a divine lark descending from the sky. History and symbol converge in this great stanza, as if an aura of beatitude surrounded the first, and the second consented to be seen. Life assumes the freedom of art, art the fullness of life. Fact, time, place, and person converge upon tree and dancer; when we say that tree and dancer are symbols, we mean that mere things are touched with supernatural radiance. Their unity is indissoluble. Symbolism has become secret history, and history is transfigured.

This is not the whole story. If it were, it would imply an order of history in which everything would know its place. There are poems which celebrate that happiness, but they are few. Normally, they are forestalled by the inveterate obstacles, division, alienation, antinomies of mind and world. Some arise from within. A constant motif in Yeats's mature poems is the question of the monstrous, the inconceivable event that humiliates history and makes nonsense of finite order. The supernatural is monstrous in a good or bad sense, because it cannot be imagined; it defeats the imagination; affronted, the imagination can only play a guessing game, hoping to come upon an approximation. It seems impossible to reconcile the inconceivable with human freedom, except by the miserable stratagem of choosing not to credit the signs. Yeats's last plays try to cope with monsters and fatality by dramatizing them; their dominant feeling is that version of the sublime which goes with terror. Yeats, as if recoiling from the idiom of freedom, virtually conspires with the evil genius of determinism, "what he would abhor if he did not desire it," since it is his opposite. In *The Resurrection* Greek accuses Syrian, "You talk as if you wanted the barbarian back," and Syrian answers, "What if there is always something that lies outside knowledge, outside order? What if at the moment when knowledge and order seem complete that something appears? . . . What if the irrational return? What if the circle begin again?"[32] According to the stage directions, the Syrian is laughing, evidently the Nietzschean laugh of violence and ecstasy, companionable noise to "The Second Coming." Christ's Incarnation was "outside knowledge, outside order" as knowledge and order were then understood:

> Odour of blood when Christ was slain
> Made all Platonic tolerance vain
> And vain all Doric discipline.[33]

Two thousand years later we expect the next "influx," and, while we have no idea what form the irrational will take, it cannot well be human.

It is customary, in glossing "The Second Coming," to refer to that passage in Book 4 of *A Vision* where Yeats, having named Henry Adams, Petrie, and Spengler as Viconian philosophers of history, offers his own prediction, an "antithetical revelation" which will come "neither from beyond mankind nor born of a virgin, but begotten from our spirit and history." It is not clear why our spirit should want such a monster, unless its lust for conflict and apocalypse is insatiable, as perhaps it is; or unless Yeats's reason is true, that we long to be cured of desire. That history is ready to give birth to a monster seems at least probable. Yeats associates with his prediction Blake's *The Mental Traveller*, presumably for its visionary grappling of opposites, male and female, birth and death: "Terror strikes thro' the region wide: / They cry 'The Babe! the Babe is Born!' / And flee away on Every side." The approaching anti-

[32] *Collected Plays*, p. 371.
[33] *Ibid.*, p. 373.

thetical dispensation, Yeats says, "obeys imminent power, is expressive, hierarchical, multiple, masculine, harsh, surgical"; it must "reverse our era and resume past eras in itself." What else it must be, "no man can say, for always at the critical moment . . . the unique intervenes."[34] The unique is the supernatural, the irrational, the monstrous. Yeats then gives, as if by doing so he would make all clear, the lines from "The Second Coming" which describe the "shape with lion body and the head of a man."

"Turning and turning in the widening gyre": the poem begins with the last act of the present cyclical drama. In his note in *Michael Robartes and the Dancer* Yeats says that "at the present moment the life gyre is sweeping outward . . . all our scientific, democratic, fact-accumulating, heterogeneous civilization belongs to the outward gyre and prepares not the continuance of itself but the revelation as in a lightning flash. . . ."[35] "The falcon cannot hear the falconer"; as Yeats says in *A Vision*, "the loss of control over thought comes towards the end." Some readers wish to translate the falconry into specifically political terms, but I think it better to have the effect ominous rather than particular, marking the first signs of loss of control, the collapse of official order:

> Things fall apart; the centre cannot hold;
> Mere anarchy is loosed upon the world,
> The blood-dimmed tide is loosed, and everywhere
> The ceremony of innocence is drowned.

Ceremony is described in the next poem, "A Prayer for My Daughter:" "Ceremony's a name for the rich

[34] *A Vision*, pp. 262–63.
[35] *Variorum Poems*, p. 825.

horn," the cornucopia of "radical innocence." When the soul, having expelled hatred, learns that it is "self-delighting, / Self-appeasing, self-affrighting," it learns also "that its own sweet will is Heaven's will," presumably because it is no longer necessary to distinguish between Heaven and itself. The "blood-dimmed tide" is the "filthy modern tide" of "The Statues." "Surely some revelation is at hand; / Surely the Second Coming is at hand": not the promised second coming of Christ, but Yeats's equivalent of the monstrous dragons in the Revelation of Saint John.

> Somewhere in sands of the desert
> A shape with lion body and the head of a man,
> A gaze blank and pitiless as the sun,
> Is moving its slow thighs, while all about it
> Reel shadows of the indignant desert birds.

This is the Egyptian sphinx, not Oedipus's riddler. I think it also comes from a trope which Yeats recalls several times in prose, the passage in the *Odyssey* where Heracles is seen by Odysseus in Hell. Heracles is present in Hell only in his shade; the real Heracles, man rather than shade, is at the banquet of the gods. Yeats ends the "Dove or Swan" section of *A Vision* with the dense question: "shall we follow the image of Heracles that walks through the darkness bow in hand, or mount to that other Heracles, man, not image, he that has for his bride Hebe, 'the daughter of Zeus the mighty and Hera shod with gold'?" Twenty years earlier he had recited the same passage, with more detail, at the end of 'Swedenborg, Mediums, and the Desolate Places':

> . . . in the *Odyssey* where Odysseus speaks not with 'the mighty Heracles', but with his phantom, for he himself 'hath joy at the banquet among the deathless

gods and had to wife Hebe of the fair ankles, child of Zeus and Hera of the golden sandals', while all about the phantom 'there was a clamour of the dead, as it were fowls flying everywhere in fear'.[36]

I suggest that the "shape" in the poem, the sphinx, is related also to Christ as phantom to man. The desert birds are flying, like Homer's fowls, in fear and terror from the new monster. "Indignant" is a touch of mastery, because it humanizes the reaction of the birds without qualifying their fright: witnesses of a new incarnation treat it with contempt as well as horror. If my reading of the passage is feasible, it clears up a difficulty that some readers have found in the last lines, the apparently pointless scandal of the impending birth of a monster at Bethlehem:

> And what rough beast, its hour come round at last,
> Slouches towards Bethlehem to be born?

It is natural that the new Galilean turbulence should begin where its predecessor began, the circle coming round again. "After us the Savage God."

It is important to keep ethical responses as far as possible away from these lines: we are dealing with a monster, so it is beyond good and evil. "A gaze blank and pitiless as the sun": "gaze" has its Yeatsian meaning, already discussed, while "blank and pitiless" removes the monster from our moral concern; it is a form of the supernatural, hence it makes our moral categories vain. The poem imagines the next eruption of the supernatural and its descent upon the natural, "the unique" bursting into history, destroying old orders. Our response to it depends upon what we make of Yeats's tone; some readers have taken it as the tone

[36] *Explorations*, p. 70.

of horror, a poet dreading the inevitable. The poem was written some months after the Great War and the Russian Revolution, and it expresses Yeats's terror at the anarchy loosed upon the world. There is strong evidence for this reading, but it does not take account of other elements in the poem, especially the Syrian note of laughter behind dread. That Yeats feared the new forces is clear; it is also true, but harder to prove, that in a full description of this fear, dread must include fascination. It is typical of his sensibility to be fascinated by what it fears, by what he would desire if he did not abhor it. The easiest explanation again is "the fascination of what's difficult," especially if we add the feeling of anticipating historical destiny, whatever dreadful form that destiny is to take. There is in Yeats, especially in his later work, a determination to leave nothing unimagined, to run toward "the unique," even though the precise form of its manifestation cannot be divined. It is a commonplace in descriptions of the sublime that the perceiver is struck by the blow of an event, driven beyond himself by the revelation, and it matters little whether the event is superb or horrifying; the force of the blow is what matters. The moral sense is astonished by the "woe or wonder" of the occasion. In "The Second Coming" the note we hear includes awe as well as dread; in a technical sense, this is Yeats's most sublime poem. In the last lines, to be specific, the moral sense which registers itself at "towards Bethlehem to be born" is astounded by the monster, and this part of the feeling is given in "slouches": the poetry acts in the clash between rough beast and Christ child; Saint John's vision is overwhelmed. This is the image which, as Yeats says, "troubles my sight," and the human burden of the poem is sustained by such amateur terms and their corresponding rhythms. The poem enacts one of the perennial forms of trouble, and this is its value. The image comes "out of *Spiritus Mundi*"; it is not merely a fiction, a deliberate gargoyle. Finding words for it, Yeats draws it into the history of his poem: the process is nearly as mysterious as that by which "the unique" interrupts the formal history of human life.

His Theater

IV

Yeats registered the tension between history and symbol in theatrical terms, mainly because he conceived of action as resolving the antinomies of consciousness and experience. He was fond of quoting Goethe's saying that we never learn to know ourselves by thought, but by action. Thought is inclined to dispose its findings in some form of dualism, but action is unitary. In 1904 Yeats wrote:

> There are two kinds of poetry, and they are commingled in all the greatest works. When the tide of life sinks low there are pictures, as in the 'Ode on a Grecian Urn' and in Virgil at the plucking of the Golden Bough. The pictures make us sorrowful. We share the poet's separation from what he describes. It is life in the mirror, and our desire for it is as the desire of the lost souls for God; but when Lucifer stands

among his friends, when Villon sings his dead ladies to so gallant a rhythm, when Timon makes his epitaph, we feel no sorrow, for life herself has made one of her eternal gestures, has called up into our hearts her energy that is eternal delight.[1]

The quotation from Blake is typical of Yeats at this period: in these essays, later collected as *The Irish Dramatic Movement*, he calls upon Ireland to live and act as if under Blake's sign. "In Ireland," he goes on, "where the tide of life is rising, we turn, not to picture-making, but to the imagination of personality—to drama, gesture." The tone is hectic. Yeats is determined that the political vacuum caused by the fall of Parnell will be filled by national feeling; literature and drama are the chosen means. He was excited by the opening of the Abbey Theatre, which he helped to found as the focus of an entire country, climax of a national drama. His early essays, and especially those which he published in *Samhain* from 1901, were attempts to provide Ireland with an artistic conscience; something to live up to, as in the early years of the Abbey, and something to be rebuked by, when the Abbey went its disappointing way. Even under Yeats's leadership the Abbey showed many bad plays; nevertheless he thought that the theater would bring national life to consciousness: he supposed that the Abbey would go its own vulgar way eventually, and he was dispirited when it did.

In "William Blake and the Imagination" Yeats distinguished between reason and imagination in much the same spirit as his distinction between picture and drama:

[1] *Explorations*, p. 163.

The reason, and by the reason he [Blake] meant deductions from the observations of the senses, binds us to mortality because it binds us to the senses, and divides us from each other by showing us our clashing interests; but imagination divides us from mortality by the immortality of beauty, and binds us to each other by opening the secret doors of all hearts. . . . Passions, because most living, are most holy . . . and man shall enter eternity borne upon their wings.[2]

Yeats is paraphrasing Blake, and the language is not entirely convincing, the wish is father to the style; but its bearing is clear. He is calling Ireland to order, that is, to energy. She is to play a role comparable to the poet's. "Somebody has said that all sound philosophy is but biography," he wrote, "and what I myself did, getting into an original relation to Irish life, creating in myself a new character, a new pose—in the French sense of the word—the literary mind of Ireland must do as a whole, always understanding that the result must be no bundle of formulas, not faggots but a fire."[3] Marshall McLuhan has pointed out, following Yeats, that passionate life does not produce subtle characters: Heathcliff is less complex than Edgar Linton. Passion obliterates difference. Yeats's relation to passion is a variant of his relation to simplicity and power, hence to the simplicity of fire. The unpopular theater that he sought, when the Abbey had made itself falsely popular, was to be a place of passion and imagination. It would have an audience, fit though few, "like a secret society," admission "by favour." It might be in London rather than in Dublin; it might be anywhere. Lady

[2] *Essays and Introductions*, pp. 112–13.
[3] *Explorations*, pp. 235–36.

Cunard's drawing room in Cavendish Square would suit, and might be turned to the secret purpose of ritual for an evening or two. Drama might be an extension of the séance. It is hard to imagine a Blake among the audience, incidentally; Yeats's later theater resuscitates the idiom of Mallarmé, with qualifying intonations from Nietzsche and from the Noh drama. Mallarmé had already provided an aesthetic for the unpopular theater:

> I believe that Literature, recovered from its source, which is Art and Science, will provide us with a Theater whose performances will be the true modern form of worship: a Book, an explanation of man, sufficient for our finest dreams. I believe that all of this is written in nature in such a way that only those are permitted to close their eyes to it who are interested in seeing nothing. This work exists: everyone has attempted it, unwittingly. There is no one, genius or clown, who has not unwittingly come upon a trace of it. To reveal it, to raise a corner of the veil of what such a poem can be, is in my isolation at once pleasure and torture.[4]

It is often said that the Noh drama was a revelation to Yeats and that it changed his theater into something rich, strange, and Oriental. But the sense of life and the sense of drama which those plays stimulated were already active in him, waiting to find an appropriate form. He always despised the bourgeois theater as he despised everything from that source; he spoke of "the succession of nervous tremors which the plays of commerce, like the novels of commerce, have substituted for

[4] Stéphane Mallarmé, *Oeuvres Complètes* (Pléiade ed.; Paris, 1945), pp. 875–76. (Translation by Denis Donoghue.)

the purification that comes with pity and terror to the imagination and intellect."[5] He quotes "solider Aristotle" here rather than, say, William Archer, but Mallarmé is closer to his interests than either. When he came upon the few Noh plays he was ever to meet, issuing from the diverse hands of Ernest Fenollosa, Tokuboku Hirata, and Ezra Pound, he received them in Mallarmé's spirit. "I have invented a form of drama," he wrote in "Certain Noble Plays of Japan," "distinguished, indirect, and symbolic, and having no need of mob or Press to pay its way—an aristocratic form." The mask and headdress to be worn "by the player who will speak the part of Cuchulain" in *At the Hawk's Well* "will appear perhaps like an image seen in reverie by some Orphic worshipper." "I hope to have attained," he says, "the distance from life which can make credible strange events, elaborate words." Masks would guard the play against theater business, nervous tremors, vulgarity of movement. Michio Ito, the Japanese dancer who inspired Yeats to this exaltation, held life beautifully at a distance, receding "into some more powerful life" than the pushing world. "The arts which interest me," Yeats wrote, "while seeming to separate from the world and us a group of figures, images, symbols, enable us to pass for a few moments into a deep of the mind that had hitherto been too subtle for our habitation."[6] The imaginative power of the Japanese plays made each play an image, a concentration of dramatic energy: the play in performance became a symbol, and was revered for doing so. As for the first Japanese audiences, "I know that some among them

[5] *Essays and Introductions*, p. 165.
[6] *Ibid.*, pp. 224–25.

would have understood the prose of Pater, the painting of Puvis de Chavannes, the poetry of Mallarmé and Verlaine."[7]

The Symbolist theory of drama, such as it was, would have served Yeats's purpose admirably, save that he had already become an equivocal Symbolist, if not a lapsed member of the faith, and that he had to accommodate the theory to his "tragic sense of life." Implicit in his commitment to subjectivity and the antithetical life was the need to present the modern predicament as tragic: "We begin to live when we have conceived life as tragedy." His idiom of drama, gesture, intensity, tragedy, and so forth could not well be fulfilled in Mallarmé's *culte* or even, strictly speaking, in the Noh plays, since the tragic situation is transcended rather than resolved there. Nietzsche provided the most powerful aesthetic of tragedy, consistent with the burden of Romantic experience. So in "Estrangement" and elsewhere Yeats associates tragedy with passion rather than with character; with self-creation—"A poet creates tragedy from his own soul, that soul which is alike in all men";[8] with ecstasy, "which is from the contemplation of things vaster than the individual and imperfectly seen, perhaps, by all those that still live." Passion "looks beyond mankind and asks no pity, not even of God."[9] In "The Tragic Theatre" he writes that "tragic art, passionate art, the drowner of dykes, the confounder of understanding, moves us by setting us to reverie, by alluring us almost to the intensity of trance."[10] What

[7] *Ibid.*, p. 236.
[8] *Autobiographies*, p. 471.
[9] *Ibid.*, p. 524.
[10] *Essays and Introductions*, p. 245.

he calls tragic ecstasy is "the best that art—perhaps that life—can give."[11] As in "Lapis Lazuli":

> They know that Hamlet and Lear are gay;
> Gaiety transfiguring all that dread.

Comedy has a low place; it is linked to character, to clashes on the surface of life, therapeutically useful at best, as when Yeats rid himself of intractable feelings in *The Player Queen* by turning them into farce.

The theory is clear, but the practice is difficult. The plays to study most closely are those in which a common aim is subject to stresses of feeling and form over a period of many years. I refer to the theatrical celebration of the Cuchulain saga, which began several years before Yeats had encountered the Noh plays and persisted long after he had received and to some extent discarded the Noh form. The Cuchulain plays are crucial in his theater because like the poems they are primarily concerned to dramatize the Hero: "Nietzsche is born, / Because the hero's crescent is the twelfth," as Yeats wrote in "The Phases of the Moon," a poem to keep in mind beside this passage from *A Vision*: ". . . of the hero, of the man who overcomes himself, and so no longer needs . . . the submission of others, or . . . conviction of others to prove his victory. The sanity of the being is no longer from its relation to facts, but from its approximation to its own unity."[12] This is virtually transcribed from Nietzsche's "Of Self-Overcoming"—"*Der Selbst-Überwindung*"—in the second book of *Zarathustra*. Cuchulain is an Irish hero, but he is also a Dionysian Superman. Nietzsche says in *The*

11 *Ibid.*, p. 239.
12 *A Vision*, p. 127.

Will to Power that man's faith in himself is sustained by the few, those of inexhaustible fertility and power. Yeats wanted his Cuchulain to play a similar role in Irish life. Lady Gregory's *Culchulain of Muirthemne* was for that reason "the best book that has ever come out of Ireland," meaning the most inspiring.

On Baile's Strand is the earliest of the Cuchulain plays, the product of Yeats's association with Lady Gregory in search of Ireland's soul. He started working on the play in 1901, finished the first version in 1903, and stayed tinkering with it for a second version in 1906. Regardless of the official endorsement of personality, the play is based upon contrasts of character, particularly Cuchulain and Conchubar. Yeats found that the presentation of the material in dramatic form brought a commitment to time and therefore to body and character. Writing to Frank Fay, who was to play Cuchulain, he referred to the source of the play, the chapter called "The Only Son of Aoife" in *Cuchulain of Muirthemne*, but he told Fay to remember "that epic and folk literature can ignore time as drama cannot— Helen never ages, Cuchulain never ages":

> I have to recognise that he does, for he has a son who is old enough to fight him. I have also to make the refusal of the son's affection tragic by suggesting in Cuchulain's character a shadow of something a little proud, barren and restless, as if out of sheer strength of heart or from accident he had put affection away. . . . Probably his very strength of character made him put off illusions and dreams (that make young men a woman's servant) and made him become quite early in life a deliberate lover, a man of pleasure who can never really surrender himself. . . .

The touch of something hard, repellent yet alluring, self assertive yet self immolating, is not all but it must be there. He is the fool—wandering passive, houseless and almost loveless. Conchubar is reason that is blind because it can only reason because it is cold. Are they not the cold moon and the hot sun?[13]

The structure depends on the contrast between the two principals: Cuchulain the tragic hero, Conchubar the pragmatic man, more an antique Roman than a Celt. Cuchulain's passion for Aoife is careless, "A brief forgiveness between opposites / That have been hatreds for three times the age / Of this long-'stablished ground."[14] As Emer says in *The Green Helmet*:

> For I am moon to that sun,
> I am steel to that fire.

Cuchulain is associated with the hawk, "one of the natural symbols of subjectivity," as Yeats later wrote in *Plays and Controversies*. To give the play greater density and reverberation, Yeats added to the two principals their counter-truths, the Fool and the Blind Man, and set them quarreling in a lower key, parody figures in relation to the main plot. The aim was to gain "emotion of multitude": in an essay of that title from the same period, Yeats says that Shakespearean drama "gets the emotion of multitude out of the sub-plot which copies the main plot, much as a shadow upon the wall copies one's body in the firelight":

We think of *King Lear* less as the history of one man and his sorrows than as the history of a whole evil time. Lear's shadow is in Gloucester, who also has

[13] *Letters*, pp. 424–25.
[14] *Collected Plays*, p. 170.

ungrateful children, and the mind goes on imagining other shadows, shadow beyond shadow, till it has pictured the world.[15]

The theory is "that there cannot be great art without the little limited life of the fable, which is always the better the simpler it is, and the rich, far-wandering, many-imaged life of the half-seen world beyond it." I read this as Yeats's version of history and symbol, fact and paradigm; the little limited life of history enlarged and sent wandering through the mind by the symbolic forces it has touched. The Fool and the Blind Man wear masks, lest our minds see nothing but character.

The play is understandable in fairly conventional terms. Conchubar stands for reason's click-clack; he is a solid bourgeois citizen, timid, prudent, with a shrewd perception of the main chance; the Blind Man is his shadow. Cuchulain is the hero of action, with lidless eyes that face the sun. The themes are those of *In the Seven Woods*; much of the feeling of the play is common to that book and the love poems in *The Green Helmet and Other Poems*. This gives the play a certain radiance and it leaves a much more vivid impression than its pedantic scheme of contrasts would imply. Yeats is using the resources of the theater, so far as he commands them, to thwart the play of commerce and its attendant vulgarity. His scheme is too deliberate to be convincing, and it is saved by what he could not prevent, the personal feeling arising from his doomed love for Maud Gonne. The same feeling is felt again in *The Green Helmet*, but it is turned to hauteur as in such poems as "No Second Troy" and "Pardon, Old Fathers." The play is called "an heroic farce," and this

[15] *Essays and Introductions*, p. 215.

is accurate, but the effect of the Red Man is to restore it to the serious heroic theme at the end:

> And I choose the laughing lip
> That shall not turn from laughing, whatever rise or fall;
> The heart that grows no bitterer although betrayed by all;
> The hand that loves to scatter; the life like a gambler's throw.[16]

This second Cuchulain play does not call for much comment, however; it is not injured if we think of it as left over from *On Baile's Strand*.

At the Hawk's Well (1916) is the first Cuchulain play written directly from Yeats's experience of the Noh. The movements of the actors "suggest a marionette," with masks by Edmund Dulac, dance by Ito, music of drum, gong, and zither. The substance of the play is still the pain of subjectivity, but the conflict is not merely the clash of prudence and passion. Imaginative energy has to reckon with the claims of domestic life and also with the enmity of the Absolute, "unfaltering, unmoistened eyes." So the play cannot be construed in terms of character; one of its achievements is to bring personality, in Yeats's usage, to the stage. There is an immediate gain in power of concentration: formally, the play proceeds not by adding one event to another but by releasing a cadence of energy, so that the fall of the cadence coincides with the end of the play. In that respect the play is a unified image. The Guardian of the Well deceives Cuchulain as she has deceived the Old Man; the deceit is embodied in the hawk dance. But the play is bluntly described by refer-

[16] *Collected Plays*, p. 159.

ence to dramatic event; it calls for description by way of rhythm, cadence, climax. The subjective Hero confronts his own vision as valiantly as he confronts the Guardian; the form of the drama is the form of self-definition. The most important discovery that Yeats made in the Noh was a form capable of gathering energy within its own movement: conflict is internal and external; no feeling is allowed to escape from the form. We are made to feel that Cuchulain contains all relevant energy within himself, and that the hawk dance merely brings out what is already implicit in the hero. The play gives a powerful impression of internal force; it is the theatrical form of self-conquest. In *A Vision* Yeats speaks of "a noble extravagance, an overflowing fountain of personal life," again of "a mind alone with the object of his desire."[17] The great achievement of *At the Hawk's Well* is a theatrical form in which multiplicity is brought to unity, scattered emotions to the unity of passion. If soliloquy could be conceived as dynamic, it would take such a form. Conflict is continuous, but it is derived from within as much as from without, from the creative joy with which the hero overcomes himself. The energy in question is free, gratuitous.

In *The Only Jealousy of Emer* this motive is directed toward Fand. Cuchulain is a phantom, a shade, dreaming back in solitude, but fixed, for the moment, at a point of age, burdened by "old memories" and "intricacies of blind remorse." Fand calls him to that condition, described in "Vacillation," in which, remorse cast out, the soul is blessed. The play enables Yeats to bring into drama all those feelings which are sustained by symbols—the spirits of the dead, the world of essence,

[17] *A Vision*, p. 128.

dreams, archetypes. But it turns, too, upon finite values: Emer's self-sacrifice, conflict between the motives which drive Cuchulain to Fand—"a statue of solitude"—and those which drive him to Eithne—"I have been in some strange place and am afraid." But the particular feeling turns upon freedom: the sense in which it is indeed free, subjective, antithetical, and the sense in which, ostensibly free, it receives the form of fatality.

The Death of Cuchulain (1938) is the last play in the cycle. By now, the Noh drama has ceased to answer every need; Yeats was no longer willing to hand over every relevant feeling to its determination within the chosen form. His relation to his own feeling is turbulent, often self-destructive. Cuchulain's story is given as a play within a play, and the external drama is enacted in the larger setting of Yeats's last poems. The play may still be understood in itself, but barely, and the last moments would bewilder an audience not attuned to the poet's late rhetoric.

It begins with a stage manager, the Old Man, speaking for Yeats, denouncing middle-class preoccupations "in this vile age." There is to be music, "the music of the beggar-man, Homer's music"; a dance, too, "Emer must dance, there must be severed heads—I am old, I belong to mythology—severed heads for her to dance before." But the dancer must be "the tragicomedian dancer, the tragic dancer, upon the same neck love and loathing, life and death": not "the dancers painted by Degas," with their chambermaid faces. (I see no evidence, incidentally, that a Symbolist dancer would be right for the occasion—Mallarmé's Loie Fuller, for instance; the dancer must respond to the impurity of Yeats's tone.) Then the play begins. Eithne Inguba has come with a message from Emer: Cuchulain must fight

Maeve's "Connacht ruffians." Cuchulain thinks that Eithne is sending him to his death, her eye upon a younger man, but it does not matter. Eithne denounces him as an old, forgiving man, lacking "the passion necessary to life"; but she has not betrayed him. It hardly matters. Cuchulain is still the Red Man's hero, and when a question of truth arises, he says like a good Nietzschean, "I make the truth!" He goes out to fight, returns mortally wounded. Aoife enters to finish him off, her hatred fulfilled. They talk of old fidelities. So that he may die upon his feet, Cuchulain fastens himself to a pillar stone with a belt, and Aoife helps him, winding her veil about him. "But do not spoil your veil," Cuchulain says. "Your veils are beautiful, some with threads of gold." The Blind Man comes in, Cuchulain's shadow from *On Baile's Strand*. Maeve has paid him to kill Cuchulain. Aoife leaves. Cuchulain does not resist; he is merely fulfilling his destiny.

There is a passage in *A Vision* where Yeats, speaking of the period between death and rebirth, says of one of its phases, the Return, that in it the spirit "must live through past events in the order of their occurrence, because it is compelled by the Celestial Body to trace every passionate event to its cause until all are related and understood, turned into knowledge, made a part of itself."[18] Nothing that happens to Cuchulain matters now, for that reason. His feeling has concentrated itself upon one limit, the vision of his next incarnation in the form of a bird:

> There floats out there
> The shape that I shall take when I am dead,
> My soul's first shape, a soft feathery shape,

[18] *Ibid.*, p. 226.

And is not that a strange shape for the soul
Of a great fighting-man?[19]

Strange or not, it is the sole object of Cuchulain's vision. "I say it is about to sing," he declares, when the Old Man kills him. The stage darkens. The Morrigu, goddess of war, arranges a dance of the severed head. Emer dances, and "a few faint bird notes" are heard. When the stage brightens, Emer has gone, the scene is modern; three musicians appear in ragged clothes, and one of them sings a harlot's song to the beggar man.

The song is difficult. There are signs that the play was not entirely complete when Yeats put it aside. "The flesh my flesh has gripped / I both adore and loathe," the harlot sings, and we recall the Old Man's dancer, "upon the same neck love and loathing." The harlot then says:

> Are those things that men adore and loathe
> Their sole reality?

and I suppose we take the question in the general setting of opposites, death-in-life and life-in-death; though it obviously comes from perturbation, as if the strategy of self and mask, long maintained, were now at a point of collapse. The questions which follow are only barely related to Heraclitean aphorisms:

> What stood in the Post Office
> With Pearse and Connolly?
> What comes out of the mountain
> Where men first shed their blood?
> Who thought Cuchulain till it seemed
> He stood where they had stood?

---

[19] *Collected Plays*, p. 444.

No body like his body
Has modern woman borne,
But an old man looking on life
Imagines it in scorn.
A statue's there to mark the place,
By Oliver Sheppard done.
So ends the tale that the harlot
Sang to the beggar-man.[20]

It is sometimes maintained, partly on the evidence of these lines, that Yeats is repudiating, once for all, the whole heroic ideal, imagining it in scorn. The evidence can be read in another way. True, Cuchulain is no longer the man of action, though he goes willingly to the fight. He is no longer interested in the external marks of heroism, because his existence is purely internal; he lives now in the dream, concentrating whatever will he has upon the next turn of his gyre. In the poem "Cuchulain Comforted" the hero, a shade among shades, is in the phase which Yeats in *A Vision* calls the Shiftings, when the spirit is purified of good and evil. "In so far as the man did good without knowing evil, or evil without knowing good, his nature is reversed until that knowledge is obtained."[21] Cuchulain obtains the knowledge by meeting his opposites, the "convicted cowards," and his comfort is in assent to the process. In the play he is heroic in the degree of that assent. Still available to the Irish as paradigm, he stands beside Pearse and Connolly in the General Post Office in 1916; they act their heroism through his. This is what comes out of the mountain, though "thought" is a poor word for the feelings which brought him forth. Pearse and

[20] *Ibid.*, p. 446.
[21] *A Vision*, p. 231.

Connolly are not shamed in Cuchulain's eyes, nor is the heroic ideal lost in him. The Old Man's scorn is visited not upon Cuchulain, Pearse, or Connolly, but upon a world which has let them down. Sheppard's statue of Cuchulain is there "to mark the spot" in the G.P.O., and without it we should have forgotten the passion that produced the Rebellion. In "The Statues," a companion poem to *The Death of Cuchulain*, Yeats asks:

> When Pearse summoned Cuchulain to his side,
> What stalked through the Post Office?

The verbs show that what stalked was heroic, super-human. The poem is more coherent than the harlot's song because it turns upon the idea of the completed symbol and finds sanction in the Grecian statues. In the play, Yeats finds an appropriate "end" for Cuchulain, in conspiring with his fate, but not for his modern audience: in the poem, a mutual end is given in the statue. In "The Mandukya Upanishad" he writes of "the dreamer creating his dream, the sculptor toiling to set free the imprisoned image": Michelangelo's labor, especially.[22] Partly, this is what Yeats tried to do in *The Death of Cuchulain*; he sets his hero free but would not give us the same freedom. This may account for the acrid tone in the Old Man's gloss; though it is clear that Yeats wanted his note to be "wild" in the special sense indicated in a late poem, "Those Images":

> Seek those images
> That constitute the wild,
> The lion and the virgin,
> The harlot and the child.

[22] *Essays and Introductions*, p. 477.

These "make the Muses sing" because they are the age-less forms of energy, lyric figures active in the human play: they are what psychology, "that modish curiosity," tries to pervert.

It is clear, when one thinks of the Cuchulain plays as a cycle, that *At the Hawk's Well* and *The Only Jealousy of Emer* are the most successful; feeling and form are indistinguishable. Everything comes together—theme, gesture, rhythm, dance. If form means achieved content, as modern critics say, these plays are formal satisfactions. *On Baile's Strand*, beautiful as it is and drawn from the same sources of feeling, has an air of existing at one remove from Yeats's deepest concerns, and the reason must be a defect of form. The play gives an impression of being a made thing, if well-made; it does not move to its own tune. In *The Death of Cuchulain* the dance form has not survived at all: like nearly everything else at this late stage—Symbolism, mask, role-playing—the form exists so that it may be abused, and most of the feeling is in the abuse. The play is remarkably powerful, as many of Yeats's last poems are, but its feeling spills out on all sides: we love it for the recklessness with which it turns against itself. A theater in which the Noh, Nietzsche, Mallarmé, and Yeats would find themselves simultaneously acknowledged would be a monster. Yeats did not devise such a thing; it may always have been a chimera. One or another personality must predominate. In that respect the most fortunate dominance was the Noh, because it enabled Yeats to "climb to his proper dark" out of the conventional theater. Mallarmé qualifies Yeats's theater, gives it a nuance of feeling not otherwise possible; Nietzsche brought turbulence, inciting Yeats to release his own.

We began with conflict, a natural point of departure

for a commentary on Yeats as dramatic poet. Then we noted Yeats's dramatic sense in relation to tragedy and ritual, his sluggish access to comedy, thinking of that form in sullen association with character, surface, mimicry, and intrigue. We should now look somewhat beyond conflict, if that is possible, to see the form of its resolution, but bearing in mind that the process is more important than the end. One of the peculiar aspects of Yeats's imagination, however, is that it readily consorts with stillness: recall how often he refers to trance when another dramatist would sound the noise of battle. Sometimes he describes trance in lively fashion—he speaks of the intensity of trance, taking the harm out of it—but the association is odd. Stillness is the end that Yeats's drama proposes; trance and silence are its forms. He writes of "that stilling and slowing which turns the imagination in upon itself,"[23] and the direction is approved: he deplored stage trappings, coming and going across the boards, because they kept the mind vainly busy. Drama should release its audience from the chains of mortality; it should speak only to make silence deeper.

This is one kind of resolution. Another is the recognition, beyond conflict, that a miracle has taken place, the divine spirits have descended to earth, and the name of the event is beauty. The First Musician's song at the beginning of *The Only Jealousy of Emer* resumes the theme in notes first heard in "Adam's Curse":

> What death? what discipline?
> What bonds no man could unbind,
> Being imagined within
> The labyrinth of the mind,

[23] *Ibid.*, p. 529.

> What pursuing or fleeing,
> What wounds, what bloody press,
> Dragged into being
> This loveliness?[24]

and in "The Phases of the Moon" Aherne tells Robartes what he does not need to be told, that "all dreams of the soul / End in a beautiful man's or woman's body." A corresponding miracle is growth, as in the flowering of a tree. In these instances the miracle is pure grace, a gift, marriage of heaven and earth: our part is to receive it. A corresponding grace may come from within, its sign the dance, "body swayed to music," an act of the imagination for which body provides the visible means. Finally, there is flame, a consummation of being which destroys being, but grand for that reason. Flame transmutes substance, changing it into a higher form, so its imagery is equally available to alchemist and lover; the flame is sexual and magical. I mention these ends not to exhaust them but to say that they are never transcendental. Yeats is determined to press the human imagination to its limit; he delights to live, imaginatively, at the end of the line. But he is never willing to release himself, once for all, from the human cycle. When he speaks of God, mostly he means that form of death which the imagination proposes as its highest limit. By symbol, he means what the imagination has taken to itself as a permanent possession. In this setting, what the theater offered him, and especially the Noh drama, was a means of registering the double conflict of life: external, the hero's war against circumstance; internal, when the hero's imagination lives by challenging itself,

---

[24] *Collected Plays*, p. 185.

one image provokes another, and energy acts within its own circle. The external conflict might have been enacted in conventional ways; the theater is rich in these. Internal conflict, on the other hand, needed something like the Noh, if not solely the Noh, and the dance is its exemplary gesture.

Of the drama in its bearing upon his life and work, Yeats has written in "The Circus Animals' Desertion," an authoritative poem on the loss of inspiration. Lacking a theme, the poet must be "satisfied with my heart," heart meaning self and the values endorsed in the "Dialogue of Self and Soul" and "Vacillation," the values for which Homer is Yeats's example. The circus animals, images and symbols which obeyed his call, are departed, and he views them in that light. Rehearsing old themes in the absence of new ones, he recalls "The Wanderings of Oisin," *The Countess Cathleen*, and *On Baile's Strand*, not in themselves but in their personal source, his desolate love for Maud Gonne. In the third stanza he refers to "a dream" brought forth from this pain, "and soon enough / This dream itself had all my thought and love." In the dialectic of Yeats's poems generally, heart or self is set off against soul or spirit; in this poem, heart is associated with old age and soul with symbol, magic, inspiration. Poetry is featured as compensation for the failure of love, and though it is called "dream" we should try thinking of it as vision, too, as in "Dream of the noble and the beggar-man"; otherwise it appears mere wish-fulfillment. By this reading, dream is related to fact as shade to person; shade, engendered by illimitable desire. Feeling, thwarted, compensates for lack by setting up a dream, a vision, a poem. And soon the dream takes all his thought and love:

And when the Fool and Blind Man stole the bread
Cuchulain fought the ungovernable sea;
Heart-mysteries there, and yet when all is said
It was the dream itself enchanted me:
Character isolated by a deed
To engross the present and dominate memory.
Players and painted stage took all my love,
And not those things that they were emblems of.

The lines are not so forthcoming as they seem. The
heart-mysteries in *On Baile's Strand* are presumably
contained in Cuchulain's heroic but crazed fight with
the waves; the personal application to Yeats's love may
be assumed. The dream is again the vision of art, at
whatever cost, and the enchantment is compensation
for the lost magic of love. But then the dream is
described: character isolated by a deed, Cuchulain's
character isolated and turned into personality, assimilated to Yeats's general idiom of lonely, antithetical
heroes. It is not clear whether the dream is the art
itself, the achievement of the play, or the image,
Cuchulain dominating memory with his great gesture.
It makes a difference. If the dream is art, then the
personal suffering is consigned to the form, the imper-
sonality of art, and passion is well spent in the work. If
it is Cuchulain, then Yeats the defeated lover is still
present and has merely translated his passion into
mythic frenzy. The last lines of the stanza move
toward art and away from Cuchulain, but the assertion
seems excessive, Yeats is protesting his "pure poetry"
too much. "Those masterful images because complete
/ Grew in pure mind," he begins the last stanza, as if
he were referring to heuristic fictions; "masterful" is
repeated from "masterful Heaven" in the third stanza,

so I assume it means that the images have the same power to save their poet's soul. Emblems, pure mind, players and painted stage; but they began from the rag bag of experience, odds and ends, casual appurtenances of "heart":

> Now that my ladder's gone,
> I must lie down where all the ladders start,
> In the foul rag-and-bone shop of the heart.

These lines have been interpreted as denoting a willing commitment to "life," even without the glow of inspiration, but I am not sure this is right, especially when I recall "the mill of the mind, / Consuming its rag and bone" from "An Acre of Grass." It is true that "foul" is often a word of praise in Yeats's poems (especially in the Crazy Jane sequence, though not in the later "Bronze Head") when the values of self or heart are dominant. The ladder is the winding stair of the tower, the climb to symbol, Platonic frenzy, inspiration. But the lines seem to me a rueful acknowledgement of the facts, not a Wordsworthian assertion that what is left will be a more substantial joy than the original.

As always, it is worth while consulting the poems before and after this one in the *Collected Poems*. Before, Crazy Jane is meditating on this vile age: last night she dreamed of Cuchulain and his Emer:

> Thereupon,
> Propped upon my two knees,
> I kissed a stone;
> I lay stretched out in the dirt
> And I cried tears down.

It is clearly relevant, one loss calling to another. In the poem immediately following, a poet, wearied of politics and noise, looks at a girl:

> But O that I were young again
> And held her in my arms!

And in the next poem, "The Man and the Echo," Yeats tries to cheer himself up, justifying his life's work while fearing that it may all be a dream. In this larger context the last lines of "The Circus Animals' Desertion" ask to be read as moral accountancy, balancing profit and loss. Yeats was always concerned with the enforced choice between perfection of the life and perfection of the work, with the relation between "the day's vanity" and "the night's remorse." Now, feeling loss which he interprets as remorse, he looks for vanity. Hence the dream, which at this stage seems precariously balanced between two meanings, illusion and vision, though leaning somewhat toward the first. In "The Gyres" Yeats leans the other way: "For painted forms or boxes of make-up / In ancient tombs I sighed, but not again."

It is perhaps surprising that Yeats's plays figure so largely in "The Circus Animals' Desertion"; he cannot have thought them as important as his poems. I think he felt that, important or not in their own right, they played a crucial part in his life. A poet who commits himself to action rather than knowledge, conflict rather than peace, is bound to seek appropriate forms in the theater. Plays are the natural culmination of Yeats's idiom: mask, role, opposites, conflict, discipline, body and soul. The theater also allowed Yeats to express his heart-mysteries while seeming to present a tale of Cuchulain, Forgael, Dectora. But the largest consideration is that the theater allowed him to devise "masterful images," starting from the bundle of accident and incoherence. The plays are therefore part of the grand intention, to make himself over again: that the images live in the realm of action means that they are unquestionable.

The Savage God

In Book 5 of *A Vision*, dated February 1925, Yeats wrote:

> A civilization is a struggle to keep self-control, and in this it is like some great tragic person, some Niobe who must display an almost superhuman will or the cry will not touch our sympathy. The loss of control over thought comes towards the end; first a sinking in upon the moral being, then the last surrender, the irrational cry, revelation—the scream of Juno's peacock.[1]

In its syntax it recalls "Leda and the Swan," in its tone "The Second Coming." The scream of Juno's peacock is heard through an entire generation. We hear it in Eliot's "The Hollow Men,"

[1] *A Vision*, p. 268.

D. H. Lawrence's *The Plumed Serpent*, Wyndham Lewis's *The Apes of God*, Pound's *Jefferson and/or Mussolini*, Yeats's *The Tower*. From a passage already quoted: "The world begins to long for the arbitrary and accidental, for the grotesque, the repulsive and the terrible, that it may be cured of desire."[2] According to *A Vision* and Yeats's last plays, the next turn of the gyre is ordained, everything yields to the cycle. "This age and the next age / Engender in the ditch." The copulation is terrible; Yeats sometimes denounces it, more often accepts it, with whatever degree of dismay, as the work of history, the price of form. As for his own role in such an age, the possibilities are limited, the most he can seek is to make himself a tragic hero or at least an actor skilled in a few tragic gestures. In many of the last poems the dominant stance is that of fierce, desperate joy, Nietzsche's tragic ecstasy; but what we feel in the lines, too, is Yeats's terrible insistence. He put those poems together to keep himself from falling apart. He insists, now more than ever, upon passion rather than knowledge:

> Empty eyeballs knew
> That knowledge increases unreality, that
> Mirror on mirror mirrored is all the show.

But boys and girls who press "live lips upon a plummet-measured face" know that passion can "bring character enough."

It is splendid, but it hardly conceals despair. Yeats's idiom is threatening to tell against him. The trouble with "consciousness as conflict" is that, when the conditions are hostile, the theatrical image dissipates itself

[2] *Ibid.*, p. 295.

in violence. Deprived of an enabling form, energy turns back upon itself, erupting because it must. In Yeats, vain energy took for the most part a political turn, and readers have felt that the poetry is saved by that exigency; the impurities run into ground already poisoned. But the question is not simple.

As for the poisoned land of politics, it is a commonplace that many of the greatest writers in Yeats's generation felt that reality had now taken a political form and that it could not be evaded in that capacity. Many of these writers, too, recoiled against the current of liberal democracy as if it were what Pound called it in the *ABC of Economics*, "a mess of mush." Their preferred values were formal, precise, hierarchical, often authoritarian; it is a painful story, and we do not understand it in full. Yeats is an extreme example. In 1937 he praised "rule of kindred" as the impending form of government, set off against the heterogeneity of the time. "Great nations blossom above," he sang in "Three Marching Songs": "A slave bows down to a slave." In the Diary of 1930 he said, "We wait till the world changes and its reflection changes in our mirror and an hieratical society returns, power descending from the few to the many, from the subtle to the gross, not because some man's policy has decreed it but because what is so overwhelming cannot be restrained."[3] He had lost confidence in the discovery of order among natural materials; order must be imposed if it is to prevail. The terminology of strong men, heroes, power is more assertive than ever: significantly, he read Nietzsche again in 1936–1937. He found justification in the history of art. The classic imposition of order was the victory of Greek statuary over Asiatic formlessness: "Europe was not

[3] *Explorations*, p. 337.

born when Greek galleys defeated the Persian hordes at Salamis; but when the Doric studios sent out those broad-backed marble statues against the multiform, vague, expressive Asiatic sea, they gave to the sexual instinct of Europe its goal, its fixed type."[4] Or the same in verse, "The Statues":

> for the men
> That with a mallet or a chisel modelled these
> Calculations that look but casual flesh, put down
> All Asiatic vague immensities,
> And not the banks of oars that swam upon
> The many-headed foam at Salamis.
> Europe put off that foam when Phidias
> Gave women dreams and dreams their looking-glass.

The many-headed foam corresponds to modern democracy, detested for its mess and vagueness.

It is also linked with racial degeneracy, "Gangling stocks grown great, great stocks run dry, / Ancestral pearls all pitched into a sty." In "To-morrow's Revolution" Yeats maintained that "since about 1900 the better stocks have not been replacing their numbers, while the stupider and less healthy have been more than replacing theirs." Sooner or later, he insisted, "we must limit the families of the unintelligent classes." Hopefully "the best bred from the best shall claim again their ancient omens."[5]

It is often held that these wretched sentiments were aroused in the bitterness of Yeats's last years and may be considered mere ash on an old man's sleeve. But their origins are much deeper in his sensibility; they return to his early sense of culture, "the inherited glory of the rich," tradition, and charm. In 1900 he transcribed

---

[4] *Ibid.*, p. 451.
[5] *Ibid.*, pp. 423, 426, 437.

from the notes to *Queen Mab* a passage in which Shelley writes of "a perfect identity between the moral and physical improvement of the human species," though Shelley's vegetarian argument in those pages cannot have pleased him much.[6] In "Estrangement" he says that "culture is the sanctity of the intellect," and by culture he means certain high products of freedom, good breeding, and wealth. One of the considerations that led him to approve of the Fascists was that their policy in regard to land had "the history of the earth to guide it, and that is permanent history." "If I till my land," he argues, "I should have rights because of that duty done, and if I have much land, that, according to all ancient races, should bring me still more rights."[7] The liaison of feeling that Yeats sponsored between peasant and aristocrat meant a paternalistic society of rights and duties based on land. Fascism had a better chance of his praise than, say, Nazism because its most spectacular version was enacted upon his beloved Italian soil and he could not help believing that somewhere beneath those marching boots one might hear the sweet sounds of Urbino, "the wise Duchess," and Lady Emilia giving the theme. So he found it easy to mistake Mussolini for Duke Frederick, Gentile for Castiglione, and to think of them in civilized association with Parnell, O'Leary, Kevin O'Higgins, and the great immortals.

That Yeats was attracted to the Fascists is indisputable. He criticized them in occasional detail, mainly because he thought them entirely wrong in sponsoring large families, but generally they caught his imagination; he seems to have traced a straight line between Fascism and old-world charm. Still, he could not be

[6] *Essays and Introductions*, p. 71.
[7] *Explorations*, p. 312.

more than a tourist in Fascist Italy. This is Pound's meaning, I think, in a passage from *Thrones*:

> But the lot of 'em, Yeats, Possum, Old Wyndham
> had no ground to stand on
> Black shawls still worn for Demeter
> in Venice,
> in my time,
> my young time.[8]

Pound is saying that the trouble with Yeats, Eliot, and Lewis in their political sentiments is that their feelings are not grounded in their soil, whereas the Fascists are expressing the genuine Italian tradition, the genius of their place. There is a lot to be said for this view, incidentally. Eliot himself warned that sound political thought in one country cannot be built upon political facts in another: for his own part, I might mention, he is on record as saying that Fascism, considered as a political faith, is humbug. In Ireland, Yeats's cordiality to the Blueshirts was certainly an attempt to sponsor an authoritarian movement that would utter "the speech of the place."

It should be remembered, however, that like other writers in his time Yeats derived a politics from an aesthetic. He did not approach politics in its own terms. So the question of "trained incapacity" arises. Veblen used this phrase to refer to a situation in which a man is prevented from seeing certain things by the fact that they are not emphasized in the grammar of his professional skill. Training in one direction makes a disability in another. It may be argued that modern writers, skilled in one way and dedicated to their own idiom, are

[8] Ezra Pound, *Thrones, 96–109 de los cantares* (New York, 1959), p. 80.

for that reason disabled in other respects, including respects readily available to less talented men. It is common in moral philosophy to derive an ethic from an aesthetic, making the good a function of the beautiful: G. E. Moore, for instance. It is equally natural to derive a politics from the same source, trading upon the demon of analogy. I have no doubt that for every position in aesthetics there is a corresponding position in politics, though I do not offer to specify one, given the other. T. E. Hulme said that Yeats attempted "to ennoble his craft by strenuously believing in supernatural world, race-memory, magic, and saying that symbols can recall these where prose couldn't"; Hulme thought it "an attempt to bring in an infinity again."[9] That such an attempt has political bearings can be assumed; if analogy fails to work in this case, it is not a resourceful demon.

Think of modern aesthetics, with politics half in mind. The single article of faith that goes undisputed in the Babel of modern criticism is the primacy of the creative imagination. It bloweth where it listeth, indisputable and imperious; it gives no quarter. In extreme versions, it concedes no rights to nature, history, other people; the world of natural forms is grist to its mill. It is strange that we have accepted such an authoritarian notion in aesthetics while professing to be scandalized by its equivalent in politics. The poet is free to deal with nature as he wishes, whatever form the imposition takes. The point is not answered by saying that a political act has immediate consequences in the lives of ordinary people while an aesthetic act is merely virtual and affects nobody. What is in question is an attitude to life, whatever we wish to say further about the relation

[9] T. E. Hulme, *Further Speculations*, ed. Sam Hynes (Lincoln, Nebraska, 1962), p. 98.

between attitude and act. The freedom conceded to the poet's imagination is fundamental in European Romanticism, represented accurately enough by Coleridge. The modern understanding of imagination assumes that order is imposed upon experience by those few exceptional men capable of doing so, that it is natural for such men to do so, as an act issues from a prior capacity. It would be possible, I suppose, to devise an aesthetic that would consort with a democratic politics, but no such aesthetic has flourished in modern literature. If you start with the imagination, you propose an elite of exceptional men; their special quality is power of vision. The relation between this elite and the masses is bound to be a critical relation, and it is likely to proceed by authority. We point in this direction when we speak of a play in terms of the hero or, as in Yeats, when everything in the drama culminates in the hero. Even when Yeats writes of ostensibly historical events, he cannot prevent the authoritarian note from sounding; it comes from the aesthetic part of his mind. In "The Tragic Generation" he describes how "somewhere about 1450, though later in some parts of Europe by a hundred years or so," men came to Unity of Being; "and as men so fashioned held places of power, their nations had it too, prince and ploughman sharing that thought and feeling." "What afterwards showed for rifts and cracks were there already," he says, "but imperious impulse held all together."[10] Now it is possible, but unrewarding, to read these sentences as historical comment; their true bearing is aesthetic, they refer to art, pattern, order, tension, form, and are best received in that spirit. "Imperious" begins as a term of

[10] *Autobiographies*, p. 291.

aesthetic power, and Yeats is then pleased to find a corresponding empire of feeling in the historical world.

Reverting to the last poems and plays: their deepest impulse begins in art, then seeps into contemporary politics. The political rant is tolerable when we receive it as a poet's rage for order, a revolt against formlessness, vagueness, mess. In "The Statues" Yeats writes:

> We Irish, born into that ancient sect
> But thrown upon this filthy modern tide
> And by its formless spawning fury wrecked,
> Climb to our proper dark, that we may trace
> The lineaments of a plummet-measured face.

"We Irish"—because Berkeley used the phrase to refute English empiricists. "That ancient sect," meaning Ireland as pre-industrial, imaginative, fantastic, oral, subjective, religious, with an implication that religion comes from caste and aspires to ritual. The filthy modern tide is an image of democratic society, the herd's success story narrated in the yellow press. "Formless spawning fury": fury, often a word of praise in Yeats, is dominated here by the violent adjectives; and "spawning," despite the "frog-spawn of a blind man's ditch," comes from Yeats's disgust at large families of puny people. "Climb to our proper dark": the verb hovers between indicative and imperative, with a touch of each. Yeats is recalling us to the values of *The Winding Stair* and *The Tower*; our dark is the dark of the soul's tower, "emblematical of the night," scorning the squalor of accident. In these lines the relation between poetry, philosophy, and politics is very close, but the dominant feeling is aesthetic revulsion. The tracing of the lineaments at the end resumes the history of artistic form from Pythagorean numbers to Blake and the "profane perfection of mankind." The faces examined are divine, Yeats says in *On the Boiler,* "because all there is empty and measured."[11] In the poem as a whole, the symbolic power to make an image, transfiguring passion as form, is focused now upon the Greek statues. I assume the image of the dancer is felt to be vulnerable, like poor Margot Ruddock, the crazed girl, "her soul in division from herself": the permanence of art must be assigned to more imperious manifestations.

It was not always so. In several earlier poems the sculptured object was seen as too remote, too bloodless to satisfy, and the dancer took all his love. Now the dancing master has outlived the dance and is in search of new employment, new analogies. Form must resist the weather of feeling, as in the statues, where calculation, number, even measurement, intellect, and passion become imperial powers set against chaos. It could be argued, incidentally, that in the politics of form, sculpture is the art most amenable to authoritarians. Music cannot forget its relation to time, the creatural predicament of rhythm and the critique of silence, despite the purity of its form. Literature is pathetically human, despite its occasional lust for the absolute. Drama cannot evade its dependence upon time, "body and its stupidity," passion and bare boards. But sculpture easily declares itself independent: it is what it is, and only the perspective of centuries can force it into time and change. A statue is not even loyal to its maker; it treats him with the same indifference that it brings to other eyes. It is significant that Yeats goes to sculpture rather than to the other arts when it is a question of "putting

[11] *Explorations*, p. 451.

down" the Asiatic vague immensities or their modern equivalents; the verb is haughty, and it comes from force. The fact that Yeats's natural art was theater, theater poetry, dramatic poetry, makes the recourse to sculpture in "The Statues" and other poems the more remarkable. In sculpture, the form stands out boldly from its setting; the political correspondence is clear. Of course this is not a full account of the situation; Yeats wrote plays virtually till the day of his death, and there are late dances, like the Queen's dance in *A Full Moon in March*. But there is, nevertheless, a turn away from body to stone, and the turn is significant—politically significant, too.

I am not trying to take the harm out of a sinister politics by calling it a post-Romantic aesthetic, but merely showing what goes with what, and the imposed order of their going. In fact, the relation between aesthetics and politics is always dangerous. In "Mr. Burnshaw and the Statue" (1936) Wallace Stevens writes of

> an Italy of the mind, a place
> Of fear before the disorder of the strange,
> A time in which the poets' politics
> Will rule in a poets' world.

But he goes on to say:

> Yet that will be
> A world impossible for poets, who
> Complain and prophesy, in their complaints,
> And are never of the world in which they live.[12]

Poets, that is to say, live by hallucination, and must do so, or their poetry dies. Walter Benjamin has argued,

[12] Wallace Stevens, *Opus Posthumous* (New York, 1957), p. 48.

speaking in the idiom of history and Marxist politics, that "all efforts to render politics aesthetic culminate in one thing: war." Fascism is his example, "the logical result of Fascism is the introduction of aesthetics into political life." "The violation of the masses, whom Fascism with its Führer cult forces to its knees, has its counterpart," Benjamin says, "in the violence of an apparatus which is pressed into the production of ritual values."[13] He maintains that Fascism is the consummation of *"L'art pour l'art,"* its motto *"Fiat ars—pereat mundus"*:

> Mankind, which in Homer's time was an object of contemplation for the Olympian gods, now is one for itself. Its self-alienation has reached such a degree that it can experience its own destruction as an aesthetic pleasure of the first order. This is the situation of politics which Fascism is rendering aesthetic.[14]

Marinetti's Futurist hymn to war is then quoted; the year is 1936, Yeats's time, but it would be fanciful to put Yeats and Marinetti in the same ideological cell. There are degrees of Fascism as of other allegiances. But the evidence in Yeats's case is strong, too. "The danger is that there will be no war," he wrote, "that the skilled will attempt nothing, that the European civilisation, like those older civilisations that saw the triumph of their gangrel stocks, will accept decay."[15] In "Three Songs to the Same Tune" he sings, "But a good strong cause and blows are delight." Sometimes he lauds war for Nietzsche's reason, that it hardens muscle, but normally he has more than muscle in view. "Desire

---

[13] Walter Benjamin, *Illuminations*, trans. Harry Zohn, ed. Hannah Arendt (New York, 1969), p. 241.
[14] *Ibid.*, p. 242.
[15] *Explorations*, p. 425.

some just war," he writes, "that big house and hovel, college and public-house, civil servant . . . and international bridge-playing woman, may know that they belong to one nation."[16] We are returned to Parnell, Mitchell, and O'Leary; only the times have changed.

Yeats is shouting in the dark. His liaison of peasant and prince is touching, and the aesthetic source from which it comes is clear, but it was always, in the limiting sense, a dream. Even in Ireland, peasant and prince were declining classes. Aristocrats were already archaic; of the few who survived, some lived in London, using Dublin for an annual visit to the Horse Show, and the remoter parts of Ireland as fishing lodges. The peasants were still emigrating from impoverished farms to the bourgeois amenity of English and American cities. Yeats's dream could only be sustained by deciding that for poetic purposes his peasants could be replaced by a pseudonymous fisherman, his prince by Duke Ercole. It was still possible to recite political lessons from Vico, Burke, and Swift, but there was little hospitality for such parables in Senator Yeats's bourgeois island. This may help to explain the stridency of his last years, the impression of a great soul at the end of its tether.

It would be strange, therefore, if Yeats's last poems and plays escaped uninjured, the phantasmagoria preserving them from danger. Frank Kermode has argued in *The Sense of an Ending* that Yeats did not take his apocalyptic predictions literally, that he was saved by his skepticism and by his still persisting relation to the syntax of common speech, the values of the vernacular. It is true. But the scars are clear, nonetheless, in the last poems and plays. Tragic joy begins to sound shrill

[16] *Ibid.*, p. 441.

in "Lapis Lazuli," the wild old wicked man is tiresome, and often "an old man's frenzy" amounts to little more than a promise to "do such things, what they are yet I know not, but they shall be the terrors of the earth." I speak harshly of this element in the last Yeats because it seems to me to humiliate the magnanimity of his greatest work, the "reality and justice" of his central poems. "My temptation is quiet," he writes in "An Acre of Grass," and we know he speaks as a Nietzschean, but we wish he had yielded to it sometimes. The stress of the last years tells upon the poetry, often producing a shrill tone which I associate with hysteria of the imagination. In the account of Phase 16 in *A Vision* he wrote that "there is always an element of frenzy, and almost always a delight in certain glowing or shining images of concentrated force: in the smith's forge; in the heart; in the human form in its most vigorous development; in the solar disk; in some symbolical representation of the sexual organs; for the being must brag of its triumph over its own incoherence."[17] We hear this bragging in "Under Ben Bulben," especially the third stanza, where Yeats writes as if unity of being could be achieved by any violent man with his temper up. The bragging is felt in the insistent rhymes and generally in the blatancy of rhythm that disfigures several late poems.

Clearly, a just balance of forces is required, and those poems in the last book which are completely realized are those in which a balance is held. The idiom of a lifetime was now in danger of collapse. Yeats comes within an ace, in these last poems, of repudiating the whole structure he has made: having made it, he can

[17] *A Vision*, pp. 138–39.

think of nothing to do but pull it down. He does not pull it down, but he makes destructive noises, growling and ranting. So he directs upon his own work the scorn and violence that he cast upon the world. When we find the poems harsh and metallic, the reason is that Yeats, making sure of his own voice, drowns every other voice: differences, opposites, qualifications are censored. Many of these poems lack what Henry James calls, in the preface to *The Lesson of the Master*, "operative irony," which "implies and projects the possible other case, the case rich and edifying where the actuality is pretentious and vain." In the fine poems the possible other case is heard, as in the dialogue of heart and dream in "The Circus Animals' Desertion." In "The Man and the Echo," echo stands in judgment, however tactfully, upon the man's soul, and the effect is like a refrain of justice, qualifying the report of mere reality. The Rocky Voice issuing from a cavern does not drown the poet's questions; rather, it sets the questions reverberating among natural forms, ancestral memories. Again in "Cuchulain Comforted" opposites meet and merge before passing to the next incarnation. In "The Apparitions" a declaration of joy is qualified by terror:

> When a man grows old his joy
> Grows more deep day after day,
> His empty heart is full at length,
> But he has need of all that strength
> Because of the increasing Night
> That opens her mystery and fright.
> *Fifteen apparitions have I seen;*
> *The worst a coat upon a coat-hanger.*

The last lines make a refrain, and several poems of this time have the voices recurring in this way; gradually, the words acquire an air of coming from a far distance, bearing age-old wisdom. Verbs become proverbs. "You can refute Hegel but not the Saint or the Song of Sixpence," Yeats said in one of his last letters,[18] and he wanted the poems to sound like tales. The images that make the Muses sing are archetypal, not psychological or accidental; they must appear permanent types rather than individuals. In "Long-Legged Fly" the refrain at the end of each stanza does what insistence fails to do in the lesser poems, holds the mind to what is permanent, while everything else changes.

In this wonderfully curial poem Yeats presents Caesar, Helen of Troy, and Michelangelo—three different modes of power—united in a central silence: Caesar in his tent before battle, the maps spread out, his eyes "fixed upon nothing"; Helen, practicing "a tinker shuffle / Picked up on a street," inconsequential, yet her mind, too, "moves upon silence"; Michelangelo, painting the Sistine roof, his hand moving to and fro, his mind moving upon silence. Many years before "Long-Legged Fly," Yeats resumed a debate in "Michael Robartes and the Dancer" on the theme of body, Robartes maintaining that "all must come to sight and touch." His evidence:

> While Michael Angelo's Sistine roof,
> His 'Morning' and his 'Night' disclose
> How sinew that has been pulled tight,
> Or it may be loosened in repose,
> Can rule by supernatural right
> Yet be but sinew.

In the fourth section of "Under Ben Bulben" the same evidence is offered in proof "that there's a purpose

[18] *Letters*, p. 922.

set / Before the secret working mind." The secret working mind is the mind moving upon silence, the supernatural right of rule attested by the silence at the heart of power. The play of silence upon words, silence upon deeds, makes "Long-Legged Fly" one of the most resplendent of Yeats's later poems, and it testifies to the extraordinary balance of feeling that he could still achieve, even in a frenetic time. In "A Bronze Head" Yeats wonders, of Maud Gonne, "which of her forms has shown her substance right." The question of "composite substance," recited from "profound McTaggart's" *Studies in Hegelian Cosmology*, leads the mind to other possibilities, but the first question is not forgotten. I think it accounts for the extraordinary delicacy of these poems, when they are delicate at all.

In "To Dorothy Wellesley," finally, the sign of balance is a style of remarkable grace: it has been censured as tumid, but I think the rhetoric is earned. The verses make a parable of the poetic imagination, but only incidentally, beginning in "moonless midnight," the time of visionary power, "our proper dark." In the first lines a poet's way with natural forms and configurations is given in the "old nonchalance of the hand," the trees becoming "famous old upholsteries / Delightful to the touch," nature amenable to man. The imaginative effort is given in physical terms: "stretch," "tighten that hand," "draw them closer." There is an answering enrichment of the imagination, "rammed full / Of that most sensuous silence of the night." "Rammed" is a word Yeats associated with Ben Jonson's use of it, "so rammed with life that he can but grow in life with being."[19] "Climb to your chamber full of books and

[19] *Autobiographies*, p. 481.

wait": thereafter, the poetic spirit is to disengage itself from accident, a movement of feeling expressed in a sequence of negatives, "No books upon the knee," "no one there," "a Great Dane that cannot bay the moon," "Nothing," "Neither Content / Nor satisfied Conscience." "What climbs the stair?" What, not who, for it is a movement away from the merely personal toward the spirit of Poetry:

> What climbs the stair?
> Nothing that common women ponder on
> If you are worth my hope! Neither Content
> Nor satisfied Conscience, but that great family
> Some ancient famous authors misrepresent,
> The Proud Furies each with her torch on high.

The Furies are the spirit of Poetry understood as Platonic frenzy and inspiration ("wait"); they can hardly be taken as having the entire history attributed to them in Aeschylus's *Oresteia*, where they begin as Erinyes, goddesses of vengeance for blood spilled, and end as Eumenides, protective and somewhat managerial spirits. Their meaning in the poem is restricted by "proud" and by the contrast with content and satisfied conscience: much of their force comes from Nietzsche, but some of it reaches far back into Yeats's poetry, with "Vacillation" as an important stage in its history. The long cadence is beautifully enriched by the delayed resolution: the penultimate line is a change of key between one grandiloquent line and another—general where the lines before and after are specific, prosaic where they are poetic and high. I do not know who the ancient authors are or how they have misrepresented the Furies, but it is hardly material; the line acts by changing the dominant poetic key without committing the mind to anything very specific. Delay, however, is crucial to the rhythm. The texture of the passage is greatly enhanced by the prosaic line which it accommodates, the "grand style" of the last line is forced to justify itself. This effect, incidentally, I read as Yeats's intimate compliment to Dorothy Wellesley, because he particularly admired this quality in her poems. In his Introduction to her *Selections* he quotes a passage from the poem "Horses," ending in the superb line, "With stripe from head to tail, and moderate ears." "No poet of my generation would have written 'moderate' exactly there," he says; "a long period closes, the ear, expecting some poetic word, is checked, delighted to be so checked, by the precision of good prose."[20] It is precisely the effect of Yeats's own moderate line. I think the whole poem is a tribute not just to Yeats's friend, or even to the spirit of poetry, but to the powers of one particular poet, author of "Fire," one of Yeats's favorite poems. I might mention, by the way, that one of the attractive features of Yeats's work in these last years— and on the whole those years are terrible—is his readiness to learn from other poets, as the short verse line of *Purgatory* is adapted from Dorothy Wellesley's poems.

But the significance of "To Dorothy Wellesley" is that it brings Yeats to his inveterate idiom, conflict, the high tension of balance: domesticity and violence, beautiful woman and the Furies. A few days after sending the poem to her, Yeats wrote again:

We have all something within ourselves to batter down and get our power from this fighting. I have

---

[20] *Selections from the Poems of Dorothy Wellesley*, with an Introduction by W. B. Yeats (London, 1936), p. ix.

never 'produced' a play in verse without showing the
actors that the passion of the verse comes from the
fact that the speakers are holding down violence or
madness—'down Hysterica passio'. All depends on
the completeness of the holding down, on the stirring
of the beast underneath. Even my poem 'To D.W.'
should give this impression. The moon, the moonless
night, the dark velvet, the sensual silence, the silent
room and the violent bright Furies. Without this
conflict we have no passion only sentiment and
thought.

He reverts to the theme:

About the conflict in 'To D.W.', I did not plan it
deliberately. That conflict is deep in my subconsciousness, perhaps in everybody's. I dream of clear water,
perhaps two or three times (the moon of the poem),
then come erotic dreams. Then for weeks perhaps I
write poetry with sex for theme. Then comes the
reversal—it came when I was young with some dream
or some vision between waking and sleep with a
flame in it. Then for weeks I get a symbolism like that
in my Byzantium poem or in 'To D.W.' with flame
for theme. . . . The water is sensation, peace, night,
silence, indolence; the fire is passion, tension, day,
music, energy.[21]

It is fitting that Yeats's account of the poem should
end with that word: for our part, it is enough if we feel
the relation between energy at the source and, in the
poem, a commanding nobility of form. T. S. Eliot said
of certain poems in *The Winding Stair* that in them
"one feels that the most lively and desirable emotions
of youth have been preserved to receive their full and

[21] *Letters on Poetry from W. B. Yeats to Dorothy Wellesley*
(London, 1940), pp. 86–87.

due expression in retrospect: for the interesting feelings of age are not just different feelings; they are feelings into which the feelings of youth are integrated."[22] In the finest of Yeats's later poems one feels, indeed, continuity between youth and age: nothing has changed, but the conditions have become more difficult, the obstacles more resolute. But Yeats's art thrives upon difficulty, spurred into song by injuries which drive lesser poets to exasperation or drink. In his greatest poems the feelings are powerful, and his mastery of them is powerful. In the theater of such poems no feeling, however sullen, is abandoned or denied. "I am content to live it all again," he says in "A Dialogue of Self and Soul." He is, in that measure, heroic.

---

[22] T. S. Eliot, *On Poets and Poetry* (London, 1957), pp. 258–59.

SHORT BIBLIOGRAPHY
INDEX

SHORT BIBLIOGRAPHY

Books by Yeats

Quotations in the text are taken from the standard collections, as listed here. In cases where British and American editions vary, page references in the footnotes are to the British editions, except for the *Collected Plays*.

The Collected Poems of W. B. Yeats. London: Macmillan, 1952. New York, Macmillan, 1956 (definitive edition).

Variorum Edition of the Poems of W. B. Yeats, ed. Peter Allt and Russell K. Alspach. New York: Macmillan, 1965.

The Collected Plays of W. B. Yeats. London: Macmillan, 1952. New York: Macmillan, 1953.

Variorum Edition of the Plays of W. B. Yeats, ed. Russell K. Alspach. London and New York: Macmillan, 1966.

A Vision. London: Macmillan, 1962. New York: Macmillan, 1961. (Reprint of the second or 1937 edition.)

Autobiographies. London: Macmillan, 1961. *Autobiography*. New York: Macmillan, 1953. 3 vols.

Essays and Introductions. London and New York: Macmillan, 1961.

Explorations. Selected by Mrs. W. B. Yeats. London: Macmillan, 1962. New York: Macmillan, 1963.

Mythologies. London: Macmillan, 1962. New York: Macmillan, 1959.

Uncollected Prose. Collected and edited by John P. Frayne. Vol. I: *First Articles and Reviews 1886–1896.* London: Macmillan, 1970.

The Letters of W. B. Yeats, ed. Allan Wade. London: Rupert Hart-Davis, 1954. New York: Macmillan, 1955.

Books on Yeats

A full list of writings on Yeats is not intended. I have given only those books that will be found most generally useful.

BIBLIOGRAPHY

Wade, Allan. *A Bibliography of the Writings of W. B. Yeats,* ed. Russell K. Alspach. 3d ed. New York: Oxford University Press, 1968.

BIOGRAPHIES

Ellmann, Richard. *Yeats, the Man and the Masks.* New York: E. P. Dutton, 1958 (paper).

Hone, Joseph. *W. B. Yeats 1865–1939.* New York: St. Martin's Press, 1962 (2d ed.).

Jeffares, A. N. *W. B. Yeats, Man and Poet.* New Haven: Yale University Press, 1948.

COMMENTARIES

Jeffares, A. N. *A Commentary on the Collected Poems of W. B. Yeats.* Stanford, Calif.: Stanford University Press, 1968.

Unterecker, John. *A Reader's Guide to William Butler Yeats.* New York: Noonday Press, 1959.

CRITICISM

Bloom, Harold. *Yeats*. New York: Oxford University Press, 1970.

Donoghue, Denis, and Mulryne, J. R., eds. *An Honoured Guest*. New York: St. Martin's Press, 1966.

Ellmann, Richard. *The Identity of Yeats*. New York: Oxford University Press, 1954 (2d ed.).

Hall, James, and Steinmann, Martin, eds. *The Permanence of Yeats*. New York: Macmillan, 1961 (paper).

Henn, T. R. *The Lonely Tower*. New York: Barnes and Noble, 1965 (paper).

Hough, Graham. *The Last Romantics*. New York: Barnes and Noble, 1961 (paper).

Jeffares, A. N., and Cross, K. G. W., eds. *In Excited Reverie*. New York: Macmillan, 1965.

Kermode, Frank. *Romantic Image*. New York: Random House, 1964 (paper).

———. *The Sense of an Ending*. New York: Oxford University Press, 1967.

Maxwell, D. E. S., and Bushrui, S. B., eds. *W. B. Yeats 1865–1939*. Ibadan, Nigeria: Ibadan University Press, 1965.

Melchiori, Giorgio. *The Whole Mystery of Art*. New York: Macmillan, 1961.

Parkinson, Thomas. *W. B. Yeats, Self-Critic*. Berkeley: University of California Press, 1951.

———. *W. B. Yeats*, The Later Poetry. Berkeley: University of California Press, 1964.

Ure, Peter. *Towards a Mythology*. New York: Russell and Russell, 1967 (reprint).

———. *Yeats the Playwright*. New York: Barnes and Noble, 1963.

Winters, Yvor. *The Poetry of W. B. Yeats*. Denver, Colorado: Alan Swallow, 1960.

SPECIAL STUDIES

Adams, Hazard. *Blake and Yeats: The Contrary Vision*. New York: Russell and Russell, 1968 (reprint).

Bornstein, George. *Yeats and Shelley.* Chicago: University of Chicago Press, 1970.

Engelberg, Edward. *The Vast Design: Patterns in Yeats's Aesthetic.* Springfield, Ill.: C. C. Thomas, 1964.

Hoffman, Daniel. *Barbarous Knowledge.* New York: Oxford University Press, 1970 (paper).

Ronsley, Joseph. *Yeats's Autobiography: Life as Symbolic Pattern.* Cambridge, Mass.: Harvard University Press, 1968.

Salvadori, Corinna. *Yeats and Castiglione.* New York: Barnes and Noble, 1965.

Stallworthy, Jon. *Between the Lines: Yeats's Poetry in the Making.* New York: Oxford University Press, 1963.

Torchiana, Donald. *W. B. Yeats and Georgian Ireland.* Evanston, Ill.: Northwestern University Press, 1966.

Vendler, Helen Hennessey. *Yeats's Vision and the Later Plays.* Cambridge, Mass.: Harvard University Press, 1963.

Whitaker, Thomas. *Swan and Shadow: Yeats's Dialogue with History.* Chapel Hill: University of North Carolina Press, 1964.

Wilson, F. A. C. *W. B. Yeats and Tradition.* New York: Macmillan, 1958.

———. *Yeats's Iconography.* New York: Macmillan, 1960.

INDEX